DOVER·THRIFT·EDITIONS

The Duchess of Malfi

JOHN WEBSTER

DOVER PUBLICATIONS, INC.
Mineola, New York

DOVER THRIFT EDITIONS

GENERAL EDITOR: PAUL NEGRI
EDITOR OF THIS VOLUME: KATHY CASEY

Bibliographical Note

This Dover edition, first published in 1999, is an unabridged republication of a standard edition of *The Duchess of Malfi*, which was first published in 1623 in England. The Note has been prepared specially for this edition.

Library of Congress Cataloging-in-Publication Data

Webster, John, 1580?–1625?
 The Duchess of Malfi / John Webster
  p. cm. — (Dover thrift editions)
 ISBN 0-486-40660-1 (pbk.)
 1. Brothers and sisters—Italy—Drama. 2. Married women—Italy—Drama.
 3. Tragedies. I. Title.
PR3184.D8 1999
822'.3—dc21   98-56455
                                                                          CIP

Manufactured in the United States of America
Dover Publications, Inc., 31 East 2nd Street, Mineola, N.Y. 11501

Note

JOHN WEBSTER (ca. 1578–ca. 1634) was born in London. His father was a wealthy merchant tailor. He married Sara Peniall in 1606 and they had several children. Much of his work as a dramatist consisted of collaborations, and revising other playwrights' work. *The White Devil* (ca. 1612) may have been the first play he wrote on his own. It was not successful, but *The Duchess of Malfi*, probably first presented in 1613 or 1614, was praised by fellow dramatists.

Webster has been criticized as a writer of melodrama, replete with evil motives and bloody murders. However, his masterpiece, *The Duchess of Malfi*, is the final example of powerful Elizabethan tragedy, written when the Puritans were excoriating dramatic representations and the courtiers of James I preferred insubstantial romantic plays.

The tragic heroine, a beautiful young widow, secretly marries for love. Her new husband, her household steward, Antonio, is of low social rank. The birth of their first child infuriates her two brothers, one of whom is a Roman Catholic cardinal and the other of whom, Ferdinand, is Duke of Calabria. At first, the brothers do not know who is the child's father. Bosola, a cynical soldier of fortune, is the tool of both brothers in their perverse campaign of mental cruelty against their sister, which ends in multiple murders.

The "great men" are thoroughly corrupt, and the play is a harrowing portrait of debased human beings torturing the innocent in return for gain. However, Webster also portrays the genuine love shared by the Duchess and Antonio; the faithfulness of Antonio's old friend, Delio, and the Duchess's waiting-woman, Cariola; and the basic decency of the courtiers. The "princely" brothers' motive for reacting with such vengeful frenzy to their sister's marriage is their desire to arrange a marriage for her to their advantage and preserve her fortune for themselves upon her death. The Duchess, like other wealthy women in the power of male relatives, was treated as salable property. The penalty for seeking a portion of personal happiness was cruel indeed.

Dramatis Personae

FERDINAND, *Duke of Calabria*
THE CARDINAL, *his brother*
ANTONIO BOLOGNA, *steward of the household to the Duchess*
DELIO, *his friend*
DANIEL DE BOSOLA, *gentleman of the horse to the Duchess* [*the malcontent*]
CASTRUCCIO
MARQUIS OF PESCARA
COUNT MALATESTI
RODERIGO
SILVIO
GRISOLAN
DOCTOR
DUCHESS OF MALFI
CARIOLA, *her woman*
JULIA, *Castruccio's wife, and the Cardinal's mistress*
OLD LADY, LADIES, AND CHILDREN
Several MADMEN, PILGRIMS, EXECUTIONERS, OFFICERS, ATTENDANTS, &c.

SCENE: *Malfi, Rome, and Milan*

ACT I

Scene I

The presence-chamber in the DUCHESS's *palace at Malfi.*

Enter ANTONIO *and* DELIO.

DELIO. You are welcome to your country, dear Antonio;
    You have been long in France, and you return
    A very formal Frenchman in your habit.
    How do you like the French court?
ANTONIO. I admire it;
    In seeking to reduce both state and people
    To a fixed order, their judicious king
    Begins at home; quits first his royal palace
    Of flattering sycophants, of dissolute
    And infamous persons,—which he sweetly terms
    His master's master-piece, the work of Heaven:
    Considering duly that a prince's court
    Is like a common fountain, whence should flow
    Pure silver drops in general, but if 't chance
    Some cursed example poison 't near the head,
    Death and diseases through the whole land spread.
    And what is 't makes this blessed government
    But a most provident council, who dare freely
    Inform him the corruption of the times?
    Though some o' the court hold it presumption
    To instruct princes what they ought to do,
    It is a noble duty to inform them
    What they ought to foresee.—Here comes Bosola,
    The only court-gall; yet I observe his railing

1

Is not for simple love of piety:
Indeed, he rails at those things which he wants;
Would be as lecherous, covetous, or proud,
Bloody, or envious, as any man,
If he had means to be so.—Here's the cardinal.

Enter CARDINAL *and* BOSOLA.

BOSOLA. I do haunt you still.
CARDINAL. So.
BOSOLA. I have done you better service than to be slighted thus.
    Miserable age, where only the reward of doing well is the doing of it!
CARDINAL. You enforce your merit too much.
BOSOLA. I fell into the galleys in your service; where, for two years to-
    gether, I wore two towels instead of a shirt, with a knot on the shoul-
    der, after the fashion of a Roman mantle. Slighted thus! I will thrive
    some way: blackbirds fatten best in hard weather; why not I in these
    dog-days?
CARDINAL. Would you could become honest!
BOSOLA. With all your divinity do but direct me the way to it. I have
    known many travel far for it, and yet return as arrant knaves as they
    went forth, because they carried themselves always along with them.
    [*Exit* CARDINAL] Are you gone? Some fellows, they say, are possessed
    with the devil, but this great fellow were able to possess the greatest
    devil, and make him worse.
ANTONIO. He hath denied thee some suit?
BOSOLA. He and his brother are like plum-trees that grow crooked over
    standing-pools; they are rich and o'er-laden with fruit, but none but
    crows, magpies, and caterpillars feed on them. Could I be one of
    their flattering panders, I would hang on their ears like a horseleech,
    till I were full, and then drop off. I pray, leave me. Who would rely
    upon these miserable dependancies, in expectation to be advanced
    tomorrow? what creatures ever fed worse than hoping Tantalus?[1] nor
    ever died any man more fearfully than he had hoped for a pardon.
    There are rewards for hawks and dogs when they have done us ser-
    vice; but for a soldier that hazards his limbs in a battle, nothing but
    a kind of geometry is his last supportation.
DELIO. Geometry!
BOSOLA. Ay, to hang in a fair pair of slings, take his latter swing in the
    world upon an honorable pair of crutches, from hospital to hospital.
    Fare ye well, sir: and yet do not you scorn us; for places in the court

---

[1]Legendary king whose punishment in the lower world was to be unable to slake his
    thirst or allay his hunger.

are but like beds in the hospital, where this man's head lies at that
man's foot, and so lower and lower.   [*Exit.*

DELIO. I knew this fellow seven years in the galleys
For a notorious murder; and 'twas thought
The cardinal suborned it: he was released
By the French general, Gaston de Foix,
When he recovered Naples.

ANTONIO. 'Tis great pity
He should be thus neglected: I have heard
He's very valiant. This foul melancholy
Will poison all his goodness; for, I'll tell you,
If too immoderate sleep be truly said
To be an inward rust into the soul,
It then doth follow want of action
Breeds all black malcontents; and their close rearing,
Like moths in cloth, do hurt for want of wearing.

DELIO. The presence 'gins to fill: you promised me
To make me the partaker of the natures
Of some of your great courtiers.

ANTONIO. The lord cardinal's,
And other strangers' that are now in court?
I shall. — Here comes the great Calabrian duke.

Enter FERDINAND, CASTRUCCIO, SILVIO, RODERIGO, GRISOLAN, *and*
ATTENDANTS.

FERDINAND. Who took the ring oftenest?

SILVIO. Antonio Bologna, my lord.

FERDINAND. Our sister duchess's great-master of her household? give
   him the jewel. — When shall we leave this sportive action, and fall to
   action indeed?

CASTRUCCIO. Methinks, my lord, you should not desire to go to war in
   person.

FERDINAND. Now for some gravity: — why, my lord?

CASTRUCCIO. It is fitting a soldier arise to be a prince, but not necessary
   a prince descend to be a captain.

FERDINAND. No?

CASTRUCCIO. No, my lord; he were far better do it by a deputy.

FERDINAND. Why should he not as well sleep or eat by a deputy? This
   might take idle, offensive, and base office from him, whereas the
   other deprives him of honor.

CASTRUCCIO. Believe my experience, that realm is never long in quiet
   where the ruler is a soldier.

FERDINAND. Thou toldest me thy wife could not endure fighting.

CASTRUCCIO. True, my lord.

FERDINAND. And of a jest she broke of a captain she met full of wounds: I have forgot it.

CASTRUCCIO. She told him, my lord, he was a pitiful fellow, to lie, like the children of Ismael, all in tents.[2]

FERDINAND. Why, there's a wit were able to undo all the surgeons o' the city; for although gallants should quarrel, and had drawn their weapons, and were ready to go to it, yet her persuasions would make them put up.

CASTRUCCIO. That she would, my lord.—How do you like my Spanish jennet?[3]

RODERIGO. He is all fire.

FERDINAND. I am of Pliny's opinion,[4] I think he was begot by the wind; he runs as if he were ballasted with quicksilver.

SILVIO. True, my lord, he reels from the tilt often.

RODERIGO and GRISOLAN. Ha! ha! ha!

FERDINAND. Why do you laugh? methinks you that are courtiers should be my touchwood, take fire when I give fire; that is, laugh but when I laugh, were the subject never so witty.

CASTRUCCIO. True, my lord: I myself have heard a very good jest, and have scorned to seem to have so silly a wit as to understand it.

FERDINAND. But I can laugh at your fool, my lord.

CASTRUCCIO. He cannot speak, you know, but he makes faces: my lady cannot abide him.

FERDINAND. No?

CASTRUCCIO. Nor endure to be in merry company; for she says too much laughing, and too much company, fills her too full of the wrinkle.

FERDINAND. I would, then, have a mathematical instrument made for her face, that she might not laugh out of compass.—I shall shortly visit you at Milan, Lord Silvio.

SILVIO. Your grace shall arrive most welcome.

FERDINAND. You are a good horseman, Antonio: you have excellent riders in France: what do you think of good horsemanship?

ANTONIO. Nobly, my lord: as out of the Grecian horse[5] issued many famous princes, so out of brave horsemanship arise the first sparks of growing resolution that raise the mind to noble action.

FERDINAND. You have bespoke it worthily.

SILVIO. Your brother, the lord cardinal, and sister duchess.

---

[2]A play upon the word "tent," which also means a bandage.
[3]A jennet was a small Spanish horse.
[4]Pliny the Elder (23–79 A.D.), Roman naturalist who authored the *Historia Naturalis*.
[5]The wooden Trojan horse, described in the *Aeneid* and the *Odyssey*.

Scene II

Re-enter CARDINAL *and* FERDINAND, *with* DUCHESS *and* CARIOLA.

CARDINAL. Are the galleys come about?
GRISOLAN. They are, my lord.
FERDINAND. Here's the Lord Silvio is come to take his leave.
DELIO. Now, sir, your promise; what's that cardinal?
  I mean his temper? they say he's a brave fellow,
  Will play his five thousand crowns at tennis, dance,
  Court ladies, and one that hath fought single combats.
ANTONIO. Some such flashes superficially hang on him for form; but
  observe his inward character: he is a melancholy churchman; the
  spring in his face is nothing but the engendering of toads; where he
  is jealous of any man, he lays worse plots for them than ever was im-
  posed on Hercules, for he strews in his way flatterers, panders, intelligencers, atheists, and a thousand such political monsters. He
  should have been Pope; but instead of coming to it by the primitive
  decency of the church, he did bestow bribes so largely and so impu-
  dently as if he would have carried it away without Heaven's knowl-
  edge. Some good he hath done—
DELIO. You have given too much of him. What's his brother?
ANTONIO. The duke there? a most perverse and turbulent nature;
  What appears in him mirth is merely outside;
  If he laugh heartily, it is to laugh
  All honesty out of fashion.
DELIO. Twins?
ANTONIO. In quality.
  He speaks with others' tongues, and hears men's suits
  With others' ears; will seem to sleep o' the bench
  Only to entrap offenders in their answers;
  Dooms men to death by information;
  Rewards by hearsay.
DELIO. Then the law to him
  Is like a foul black cobweb to a spider,—
  He makes it his dwelling and a prison
  To entangle those shall feed him.
ANTONIO. Most true:
  He never pays debts unless they be shrewd turns,
  And those he will confess that he doth owe.
  Last, for his brother there, the cardinal,
  They that do flatter him most say oracles
  Hang at his lips; and verily I believe them,

For the devil speaks in them.
But for their sister, the right noble duchess,
You never fixed your eye on three fair medals
Cast in one figure, of so different temper.
For her discourse, it is so full of rapture,
You only will begin then to be sorry
When she doth end her speech, and wish, in wonder,
She held it less vain-glory to talk much,
Than your penance to hear her: whilst she speaks,
She throws upon a man so sweet a look,
That it were able to raise one to a galliard[6]
That lay in a dead palsy, and to dote
On that sweet countenance; but in that look
There speaketh so divine a continence
As cuts off all lascivious and vain hope.
Her days are practised in such noble virtue,
That sure her nights, nay, more, her very sleeps,
Are more in Heaven than other ladies' shrifts.
Let all sweet ladies break their flattering glasses,
And dress themselves in her.
DELIO. Fie, Antonio,
  You play the wire-drawer with her commendations.
ANTONIO. I'll case the picture up: only thus much;
  All her particular worth grows to this sum,—
  She stains the time past, lights the time to come.
CARIOLA. You must attend my lady in the gallery,
  Some half an hour hence.
ANTONIO. I shall.

  Exeunt ANTONIO *and* DELIO.

FERDINAND. Sister, I have a suit to you.
DUCHESS. To me, sir?
FERDINAND. A gentleman here, Daniel de Bosola,
  One that was in the galleys—
DUCHESS. Yes, I know him.
FERDINAND. A worthy fellow he is: pray, let me entreat for
  The provisorship of your horse.[7]
DUCHESS. Your knowledge of him
  Commends him and prefers him.
FERDINAND. Call him hither.

---

[6]A dance.
[7]Stewardship of her horses.

Exit ATTENDANT.

We are now upon parting. Good Lord Silvio,
Do us commend to all our noble friends
At the leaguer.[8]
SILVIO. Sir, I shall.
FERDINAND. You are for Milan?
SILVIO. I am.
DUCHESS. Bring the caroches.[9] We'll bring you down to the haven.

Exeunt DUCHESS, SILVIO, CASTRUCCIO, RODERIGO, GRISOLAN,
CARIOLA, JULIA, *and* ATTENDANTS.

CARDINAL. Be sure you entertain that Bosola
For your intelligence: I would not be seen in 't;
And therefore many times I have slighted him
When he did court our furtherance, as this morning.
FERDINAND. Antonio, the great-master of her household,
Had been far fitter.
CARDINAL. You are deceived in him:
His nature is too honest for such business.—
He comes: I'll leave you.   [*Exit*

Re-enter BOSOLA.

BOSOLA. I was lured to you.
FERDINAND. My brother, here, the cardinal, could never
Abide you.
BOSOLA. Never since he was in my debt.
FERDINAND. May be some oblique character in your face
Made him suspect you.
BOSOLA. Doth he study physiognomy?
There's no more credit to be given to the face
Than to a sick man's urine, which some call
The physician's whore because she cozens him.
He did suspect me wrongfully.
FERDINAND. For that
You must give great men leave to take their times.
Distrust doth cause us seldom be deceived:
You see the oft shaking of the cedar-tree
Fastens it more at root.
BOSOLA. Yet, take heed;

---

[8]Camp; from the German *Lager*.
[9]Stately carriages.

For to suspect a friend unworthily
Instructs him the next way to suspect you,
And prompts him to deceive you. \june

FERDINAND. There's gold.

BOSOLA. So:
What follows? never rained such showers as these
Without thunderbolts i' the tail of them: whose throat must I cut?

FERDINAND. Your inclination to shed blood rides post
Before my occasion to use you. I give you that
To live i' the court here, and observe the duchess;
To note all the particulars of her havior,
What suitors do solicit her for marriage,
And whom she best affects. She's a young widow:
I would not have her marry again.

BOSOLA. No, sir?

FERDINAND. Do not you ask the reason; but be satisfied
I say I would not.

BOSOLA. It seems you would create me
One of your familiars.

FERDINAND. Familiar! what's that?

BOSOLA. Why, a very quaint invisible devil in flesh,
An intelligencer.

FERDINAND. Such a kind of thriving thing
I would wish thee; and ere long thou mayest arrive
At a higher place by 't.

BOSOLA. Take your devils,
Which hell calls angels, these cursed gifts would make
You a corrupter, me an impudent traitor;
And should I take these, they'd take me to hell.

FERDINAND. Sir, I'll take nothing from you that I have given:
There is a place that I procured for you
This morning, the provisorship o' the horse;
Have you heard on 't?

BOSOLA. No.

FERDINAND. 'Tis yours: is 't not worth thanks?

BOSOLA. I would have you curse yourself now, that your bounty
(Which makes men truly noble) e'er should make me
A villain. O, that to avoid ingratitude
For the good deed you have done me, I must do
All the ill man can invent! Thus the devil
Candies all sins o'er; and what Heaven terms vile,
That names he complimental.

FERDINAND. Be yourself;

Keep your old garb of melancholy; 'twill express
You envy those that stand above your reach,
Yet strive not to come near 'em: this will gain
Access to private lodgings, where yourself
May, like a politic dormouse—
BOSOLA. As I have seen some
Feed in a lord's dish, half asleep, not seeming
To listen to any talk; and yet these rogues
Have cut his throat in a dream. What's my place?
The provisorship o' the horse? say, then, my corruption
Grew out of horse-dung: I am your creature.
FERDINAND. Away!
BOSOLA. Let good men, for good deeds, covet good fame,
Since place and riches oft are bribes of shame:
Sometimes the devil doth preach.   [Exit

Re-enter DUCHESS, CARDINAL, *and* CARIOLA.

CARDINAL. We are to part from you; and your own discretion
Must now be your director.
FERDINAND. You are a widow:
You know already what man is; and therefore
Let not youth, high promotion, eloquence—
CARDINAL. No,
Nor any thing without the addition, honor,
Sway your high blood.
FERDINAND. Marry! they are most luxurious[10]
Will wed twice.
CARDINAL. O, fie!
FERDINAND. Their livers are more spotted
Than Laban's sheep.
DUCHESS. Diamonds are of most value,
They say, that have passed through most jewelers' hands.
FERDINAND. Whores by that rule are precious.
DUCHESS. Will you hear me?
I'll never marry.
CARDINAL. So most widows say;
But commonly that motion lasts no longer
Than the turning of an hour-glass: the funeral sermon
And it end both together.
FERDINAND. Now hear me:
You live in a rank pasture, here, i' the court;

---

[10]Lecherous.

There is a kind of honey-dew that's deadly;
'Twill poison your fame; look to 't: be not cunning;
For they whose faces do belie their hearts
Are witches ere they arrive at twenty years,
Ay, and give the devil suck.

DUCHESS. This is terrible good counsel.

FERDINAND. Hypocrisy is woven of a fine small thread,
Subtler than Vulcan's engine:[11] yet, believe 't,
Your darkest actions, nay, your privat'st thoughts,
Will come to light.

CARDINAL. You may flatter yourself,
And take your own choice; privately be married
Under the eaves of night—

FERDINAND. Think 't the best voyage
That e'er you made; like the irregular crab,
Which, though 't goes backward, thinks that it goes right
Because it goes its own way; but observe,
Such weddings may more properly be said
To be executed than celebrated.

CARDINAL. The marriage night
Is the entrance into some prison.

FERDINAND. And those joys,
Those lustful pleasures, are like heavy sleeps
Which do fore-run man's mischief.

CARDINAL. Fare you well.
Wisdom begins at the end: remember it.   [*Exit*

DUCHESS. I think this speech between you both was studied,
It came so roundly off.

FERDINAND. You are my sister;
This was my father's poniard, do you see?
I'd be loth to see 't look rusty, 'cause 'twas his.
I would have you give o'er these chargeable revels:
A visor and a mask are whispering-rooms
That were never built for goodness;—fare ye well;—
And women like that part which, like the lamprey,
Hath never a bone in 't.

DUCHESS. Fie, sir!

FERDINAND. Nay,
I mean the tongue; variety of courtship:
What cannot a neat knave with a smooth tale
Make a woman believe? Farewell, lusty widow   [*Exit*

Cardinal & Ferdinand don't want her to marry so they can get her inheritance.

---

[11]The net that held Mars and Venus.

DUCHESS. Shall this move me? If all my royal kindred
   Lay in my way unto this marriage,
   I'd make them my low footsteps: and even now,
   Even in this hate, as men in some great battles,
   By apprehending danger, have achieved
   Almost impossible actions (I have heard soldiers say so),
   So I through frights and threatenings will assay
   This dangerous venture. Let old wives report
   I winked and chose a husband.—Cariola,
   To thy known secrecy I have given up
   More than my life—my fame.
CARIOLA. Both shall be safe;
   For I'll conceal this secret from the world
   As warily as those that trade in poison
   Keep poison from their children.
DUCHESS. Thy protestation
   Is ingenious and hearty: I believe it.
   Is Antonio come?
CARIOLA. He attends you.
DUCHESS. Good, dear soul,
   Leave me; but place thyself behind the arras,
   Where thou may'st overhear us. Wish me good speed;
   For I am going into a wilderness
   Where I shall find nor path nor friendly clue
   To be my guide.   [CARIOLA *goes behind the arras*[12]

Enter ANTONIO.

   I sent for you: sit down;
   Take pen and ink, and write: are you ready?
ANTONIO. Yes.
DUCHESS. What did I say?
ANTONIO. That I should write somewhat.
DUCHESS. O, I remember.
   After these triumphs and this large expense,
   It's fit, like thrifty husbands, we inquire
   What's laid up for to-morrow.
ANTONIO. So please your beauteous excellence.
DUCHESS. Beauteous!
   Indeed, I thank you: I look young for your sake;
   You have ta'en my cares upon you.
ANTONIO. I'll fetch your grace

---

[12]Tapestry screen.

The particulars of your revenue and expense.
DUCHESS. O, you are
  An upright treasurer: but you mistook;
  For when I said I meant to make inquiry
  What's laid up for to-morrow, I did mean
  What's laid up yonder for me.
ANTONIO. Where?
DUCHESS. In Heaven.
  I am making my will (as 'tis fit princes should,
  In perfect memory), and, I pray, sir, tell me,
  Were not one better make it smiling, thus,
  Than in deep groans and terrible ghastly looks,
  As if the gifts we parted with procured
  That violent distraction?
ANTONIO. O, much better.
DUCHESS. If I had a husband now, this care were quit:
  But I intend to make you overseer.
  What good deed shall we first remember? say.
ANTONIO. Begin with that first good deed began i' the world
  After man's creation, the sacrament of marriage:
  I'd have you first provide for a good husband;
  Give him all.
DUCHESS. All!
ANTONIO. Yes, your excellent self.
DUCHESS. In a winding-sheet?
ANTONIO. In a couple.
DUCHESS. Saint Winifred, that were a strange will!
ANTONIO. 'Twere stranger if there were no will in you
  To marry again.
DUCHESS. What do you think of marriage?
ANTONIO. I take 't, as those that deny purgatory,
  It locally contains or Heaven or hell;
  There's no third place in 't.
DUCHESS. How do you affect it?
ANTONIO. My banishment, feeding my melancholy,
  Would often reason thus.
DUCHESS. Pray, let's hear it.
ANTONIO. Say a man never marry, nor have children,
  What takes that from him? only the bare name
  Of being a father, or the weak delight
  To see the little wanton ride a-cock-horse
  Upon a painted stick, or hear him chatter
  Like a taught starling.

[handwritten margin note: marriage could be heaven or it could be hell]

DUCHESS. Fie, fie, what's all this?
  One of your eyes is blood-shot; use my ring to 't,
  They say 'tis very sovereign: 'twas my wedding-ring.
  And I did vow never to part with it
  But to my second husband.
ANTONIO. You have parted with it now.
DUCHESS. Yes, to help your eye-sight.
ANTONIÓ. You have made me stark blind.
DUCHESS. How?
ANTONIO. There is a saucy and ambitious devil
  Is dancing in this circle.
DUCHESS. Remove him.
ANTONIO. How?
DUCHESS. There needs small conjuration, when your finger
  May do it: thus; is it fit?
                          [*She puts the ring upon his finger; he kneels*
ANTONIO. What said you?
DUCHESS. Sir,
  This goodly roof of yours is too low built;
  I cannot stand upright in 't nor discourse,
  Without I raise it higher: raise yourself;
  Or, if you please, my hand to help you: so.   [*Raises him*
ANTONIO. Ambition, madam, is a great man's madness,
  That is not kept in chains and close-pent rooms,
  But in fair lightsome lodgings, and is girt
  With the wild noise of prattling visitants,
  Which makes it lunatic beyond all cure.
  Conceive not I am so stupid but I aim
  Whereto your favors tend: but he's a fool
  That, being a-cold, would thrust his hands i' the fire
  To warm them.
DUCHESS. So, now the ground's broke,
  You may discover what a wealthy mine
  I make you lord of.
ANTONIO. O my unworthiness!
DUCHESS. You were ill to sell yourself:
  This darkening of your worth is not like that
  Which tradesmen use i' the city; their false lights
  Are to rid bad wares off: and I must tell you,
  If you will know where breathes a complete man
  (I speak it without flattery), turn your eyes,
  And progress through yourself.
ANTONIO. Were there nor Heaven nor hell,

I would be honest: I have long served virtue,
And ne'er ta'en wages of her.
DUCHESS. Now she pays it.
The misery of us that are born great!
We are forced to woo, because none dare woo us;
And as a tyrant doubles with his words,
And fearfully equivocates, so we
Are forced to express our violent passions
In riddles and in dreams, and leave the path
Of simple virtue, which was never made
To seem the thing it is not. Go, go brag
You have left me heartless; mine is in your bosom:
I hope 'twill multiply love there. You do tremble:
Make not your heart so dead a piece of flesh,
To fear more than to love me. Sir, be confident:
What is 't distracts you? This is flesh and blood, sir;
'Tis not the figure cut in alabaster
Kneels at my husband's tomb. Awake, awake, man!
I do here put off all vain ceremony,
And only do appear to you a young widow
That claims you for her husband, and, like a widow,
I use but half a blush in 't.
ANTONIO. Truth speak for me;
I will remain the constant sanctuary
Of your good name.
DUCHESS. I thank you, gentle love:
And 'cause you shall not come to me in debt,
Being now my steward, here upon your lips
I sign your *Quietus est*.[13] This you should have begged now:
I have seen children oft eat sweetmeats thus,
As fearful to devour them too soon.
ANTONIO. But for your brothers?
DUCHESS. Do not think of them:
All discord without this circumference
Is only to be pitied, and not feared:
Yet, should they know it, time will easily
Scatter the tempest.
ANTONIO. These words would be mine,
And all the parts you have spoke, if some part of it
Would not have savored flattery.

---

[13]Discharge.

DUCHESS. Kneel.

CARIOLA *comes from behind the arras.*

ANTONIO. Ha!
DUCHESS. Be not amazed; this woman's of my counsel:
I have heard lawyers say, a contract in a chamber
Per verba presenti is absolute marriage.

She and ANTONIO *kneel.*

Bless, Heaven, this sacred gordian, which let violence
Never untwine! —foreshadowing
ANTONIO. And may our sweet affections, like the spheres,
Be still in motion!
DUCHESS. Quickening, and make
The like soft music!
ANTONIO. That we may imitate the loving palms,
Best emblem of a peaceful marriage,
That never bore fruit, divided!
DUCHESS. What can the church force more?
ANTONIO. That fortune may not know an accident,
Either of joy or sorrow, to divide
Our fixèd wishes!
DUCHESS. How can the church build faster?
We now are man and wife, and 'tis the church
That must but echo this.—Maid, stand apart:
I now am blind.
ANTONIO. What's your conceit in this?
DUCHESS. I would have you lead your fortune by the hand
Unto your marriage bed
(You speak in me this, for we now are one):
We'll only lie, and talk together, and plot
To appease my humorous[14] kindred; and if you please,
Like the old tale in Alexander and Lodowick,[15]
Lay a naked sword between us, keep us chaste.
O, let me shroud my blushes in your bosom,
Since 'tis the treasury of all my secrets!

Exeunt DUCHESS *and* ANTONIO.

---

[14]Having "humors" or moods.
[15]The heroes of an English ballad based on the medieval tale *Amis and Amiloun*; extraordinarily faithful friends who look alike. One friend marries a princess in behalf of the other but places a naked sword between himself and the bride in the marriage bed.

CARIOLA. Whether the spirit of greatness or of woman
Reign most in her, I know not; but it shows
A fearful madness: I owe her much of pity.   [*Exit*

ACT II

Scene I

An apartment in the palace of the DUCHESS.

Enter BOSOLA *and* CASTRUCCIO.

BOSOLA. You say you would fain be taken for an eminent courtier?

CASTRUCCIO. 'Tis the very main of my ambition.

BOSOLA. Let me see: you have a reasonable good face for 't already, and your nightcap expresses your ears sufficient largely. I would have you learn to twirl the strings of your band with a good grace, and in a set speech, at the end of every sentence, to hum three or four times, or blow your nose till it smart again, to recover your memory. When you come to be a president in criminal causes, if you smile upon a prisoner, hang him, but if you frown upon him and threaten him, let him be sure to scape the gallows.

CASTRUCCIO. I would be a very merry president.

BOSOLA. Do not sup o' nights; 'twill beget you an admirable wit.

CASTRUCCIO. Rather it would make me have a good stomach to quarrel; for they say, your roaring boys[16] eat meat seldom, and that makes them so valiant. But how shall I know whether the people take me for an eminent fellow?

BOSOLA. I will teach a trick to know it: give out you lie a-dying, and if you hear the common people curse you, be sure you are taken for one of the prime nightcaps.[17] [*Enter an* OLD LADY] You come from painting now.

OLD LADY. From what?

BOSOLA. Why, from your scurvy face-physic. To behold thee not

---

[16]Bullies.
[17]Lawyers.

painted inclines somewhat near a miracle; these in thy face here were deep ruts and foul sloughs the last progress.[18] There was a lady in France that, having had the small-pox, flayed the skin off her face to make it more level; and whereas before she looked like a nutmeg-grater, after she resembled an abortive hedge-hog.

OLD LADY. Do you call this painting?

BOSOLA. No, no, but you call it careening of an old morphewed lady, to make her disembogue[19] again: there's rough-cast phrase to your plastic.

OLD LADY. It seems you are well acquainted with my closet.

BOSOLA. One would suspect it for a shop of witchcraft, to find in it the fat of serpents, spawn of snakes, Jews' spittle, and their young children's ordure; and all these for the face. I would sooner eat a dead pigeon taken from the soles of the feet of one sick of the plague than kiss one of you fasting. Here are two of you, whose sin of your youth is the very patrimony of the physician; makes him renew his foot-cloth with the spring, and change his high-priced courtezan with the fall of the leaf. I do wonder you do not loathe yourselves. Observe my meditation now.

What thing is in this outward form of man
To be beloved? We account it ominous,
If nature do produce a colt, or lamb,
A fawn, or goat, in any limb resembling
A man, and fly from 't as a prodigy:
Man stands amazed to see his deformity
In any other creature but himself.
But in our own flesh, though we bear diseases
Which have their true names only ta'en from beasts,—
As the most ulcerous wolf and swinish measle,—
Though we are eaten up of lice and worms,
And though continually we bear about us
A rotten and dead body, we delight
To hide it in rich tissue: all our fear,
Nay, all our terror, is lest our physician
Should put us in the ground to be made sweet.—
Your wife's gone to Rome: you two couple, and get you to the wells at Lucca to recover your aches. I have other work on foot.

Exeunt CASTRUCCIO *and* OLD LADY.

I observe our duchess
Is sick a-days, she pukes, her stomach seethes,
The fins of her eye-lids look most teeming blue,

---

[18]As though a state procession had driven across it.
[19]Morphewed: scaly; disembogue: empty.

She wanes i' the cheek, and waxes fat i' the flank,
And, contrary to our Italian fashion,
Wears a loose-bodied gown: there's somewhat in 't.
I have a trick may chance discover it,
A pretty one; I have bought some apricocks,
The first our spring yields.

Enter ANTONIO *and* DELIO.

DELIO. And so long since married!
You amaze me.
ANTONIO. Let me seal your lips for ever:
For, did I think that any thing but the air
Could carry these words from you, I would wish
You had no breath at all.—Now, sir, in your contemplation?
You are studying to become a great wise fellow.
BOSOLA. O, sir, the opinion of wisdom is a foul tether that runs all over
a man's body: if simplicity direct us to have no evil, it directs us to a
happy being; for the subtlest folly proceeds from the subtlest wisdom:
let me be simply honest.
ANTONIO. I do understand your inside.
BOSOLA. Do you so?
ANTONIO. Because you would not seem to appear to the world
Puffed up with your preferment, you continue
This out-of-fashion melancholy: leave it, leave it.
BOSOLA. Give me leave to be honest in any phrase, in any compliment
whatsoever. Shall I confess myself to you? I look no higher than I can
reach: they are the gods that must ride on winged horses. A lawyer's
mule of a slow pace will both suit my disposition and business; for,
mark me, when a man's mind rides faster than his horse can gallop,
they quickly both tire.
ANTONIO. You would look up to Heaven, but I think
The devil, that rules i' the air, stands in your light.
BOSOLA. O, sir, you are lord of the ascendant, chief man with the
duchess; a duke was your cousin-german[20] removed. Say you are lin-
eally descended from King Pepin, or he himself, what of this? search
the heads of the greatest rivers in the world, you shall find them but
bubbles of water. Some would think the souls of princes were
brought forth by some more weighty cause than those of meaner persons: they are deceived, there's the same hand to them; the like passions sway them; the same reason that makes a vicar to go to law for
a tithe-pig, and undo his neighbors, makes them spoil a whole
province, and batter down goodly cities with the cannon.

---

[20]First cousin.

Enter DUCHESS *and* LADIES.

DUCHESS. Your arm, Antonio: do I not grow fat? ✓ *she's pregnant*
  I am exceeding short-winded.—Bosola,
  I would have you, sir, provide for me a litter;
  Such a one as the Duchess of Florence rode in.
BOSOLA. The duchess used one when she was great with child.
DUCHESS. I think she did.—Come hither, mend my ruff;
  Here, when? thou art such a tedious lady; and
  Thy breath smells of lemon-pills; would thou hadst done!
  Shall I swoon under thy fingers! I am
  So troubled with the mother![21]
BOSOLA. [*Aside*] I fear too much.
DUCHESS. I have heard you say that the French courtiers
  Wear their hats on 'fore the king.
ANTONIO. I have seen it.
DUCHESS. In the presence?
ANTONIO. Yes.
DUCHESS. Why should not we bring up that fashion!
  'Tis ceremony more than duty that consists
  In the removing of a piece of felt:
  Be you the example to the rest o' the court;
  Put on your hat first.
ANTONIO. You must pardon me:
  I have seen, in colder countries than in France,
  Nobles stand bare to the prince; and the distinction
  Methought showed reverently.
BOSOLA. I have a present for your grace.
DUCHESS. For me, sir?
BOSOLA. Apricocks, madam.
DUCHESS. O, sir, where are they?
  I have heard of none to-year.
BOSOLA. [*Aside*] Good; her color rises.
DUCHESS. Indeed, I thank you: they are wondrous fair ones.
  What an unskilful fellow is our gardener!
  We shall have none this month.
BOSOLA. Will not your grace pare them?
DUCHESS. No: they taste of musk, methinks; indeed they do.
BOSOLA. I know not: yet I wish your grace had pared 'em.
DUCHESS. Why?
BOSOLA. I forgot to tell you, the knave gardener,

---

[21]The effects of female hormones.

Only to raise his profit by them the sooner,
Did ripen them in horse-dung.
DUCHESS. O, you jest—
You shall judge: pray taste one.
ANTONIO. Indeed, madam,
I do not love the fruit.
DUCHESS. Sir, you are loth
To rob us of our dainties: 'tis a delicate fruit;
They say they are restorative.
BOSOLA. 'Tis a pretty art,
This grafting.
DUCHESS. 'Tis so; bettering of nature.
BOSOLA. To make a pippin grow upon a crab,
A damson[22] on a blackthorn.—[Aside] How greedily she eats them!
A whirlwind strike off these bawd farthingales![23]
For, but for that and the loose-bodied gown,
I should have discovered apparently
The young springal[24] cutting a caper in her belly.
DUCHESS. I thank you, Bosola: they are right good ones,
If they do not make me sick.
ANTONIO. How now, madam!
DUCHESS. This green fruit and my stomach are not friends:
How they swell me!
BOSOLA. [Aside] Nay, you are too much swelled already.
DUCHESS. O, I am in an extreme cold sweat!
BOSOLA. I am very sorry.
DUCHESS. Lights to my chamber!—O good Antonio, I fear I am
undone!
DELIO. Lights there, lights!

Exeunt DUCHESS and LADIES.—Exit, on the other side, BOSOLA.

ANTONIO. O my trusty Delio, we are lost!
I fear she's fall'n in labor; and there's left
No time for her remove.
DELIO. Have you prepared
Those ladies to attend her? and procured
That politic safe conveyance for the midwife
Your duchess plotted?
ANTONIO. I have.

---

[22]Plum.
[23]Hooped petticoats.
[24]Stripling, young man.

DELIO. Make use, then, of this forced occasion:
  Give out that Bosola hath poisoned her
  With these apricocks; that will give some color
  For her keeping close.
ANTONIO. Fie, fie, the physicians
  Will then flock to her.
DELIO. For that you may pretend
  She'll use some prepared antidote of her own,
  Lest the physicians should re-poison her.
ANTONIO. I am lost in amazement: I know not what to think on 't.
                                                      [*Exeunt*

Scene II

A hall in the same palace.

Enter BOSOLA.

BOSOLA. So, so, there's no question but her techiness and most vulturous eating of the apricocks are apparent signs of breeding.

Enter an OLD LADY.

OLD LADY. Now? I am in haste, sir.
BOSOLA. There was a young waiting-woman had a monstrous desire to see the glass-house—
OLD LADY. Nay, pray let me go.
BOSOLA. And it was only to know what strange instrument it was should swell up a glass to the fashion of a woman's belly.
OLD LADY. I will hear no more of the glass-house. You are still abusing women?
BOSOLA. Who, I? no; only, by the way now and then, mention your frailties. The orange-tree bears ripe and green fruit and blossoms all together; and some of you give entertainment for pure love, but more for more precious reward. The lusty spring smells well; but drooping autumn tastes well. If we have the same golden showers that rained in the time of Jupiter the thunderer, you have the same Danaës[25] still, to hold up their laps to receive them. Didst thou never study the mathematics?
OLD LADY. What's that, sir?

---

[25]Jupiter (or Zeus) wooed the maiden Danaë by transforming himself into a golden shower, which dropped into her lap.

BOSOLA. Why to know the trick how to make a many lines meet in one centre. Go, go, give your foster-daughters good counsel: tell them, that the devil takes delight to hang at a woman's girdle, like a false rusty watch, that she cannot discern how the time passes.

Exit OLD LADY. *Enter* ANTONIO, DELIO, RODERIGO, *and* GRISOLAN.

ANTONIO. Shut up the court-gates.
RODERIGO. Why, sir? what's the danger?
ANTONIO. Shut up the posterns presently, and call
  All the officers o' the court.
GRISOLAN. I shall instantly.   [*Exit*
ANTONIO. Who keeps the key o' the park-gate?
RODERIGO. Forobosco.
ANTONIO. Let him bring 't presently.

Re-enter GRISOLAN *with* SERVANTS.

1ST SERVANT. O, gentlemen o' the court, the foul treason!
BOSOLA. [*Aside*] If that these apricocks should be poisoned now,
  Without my knowledge!
1ST SERVANT. There was taken even now a Switzer[26] in the duchess's
  bed-chamber—
2ND SERVANT. A Switzer!
1ST SERVANT. With a pistol in his great cod-piece.[27]
BOSOLA. Ha, ha, ha!
1ST SERVANT. The cod-piece was the case for 't.
2ND SERVANT. There was a cunning traitor: who would have searched
  his cod-piece?
1ST SERVANT. True, if he had kept out of the ladies' chambers: and all
  the moulds of his buttons were leaden bullets.
2ND SERVANT. O wicked cannibal! a firelock in 's cod-piece!
1ST SERVANT. 'Twas a French plot, upon my life.
2ND SERVANT. To see what the devil can do!
ANTONIO. Are all the officers here?
SERVANTS. We are.
ANTONIO. Gentlemen,
  We have lost much plate you know; and but this evening
  Jewels, to the value of four thousand ducats,
  Are missing in the duchess's cabinet.
  Are the gates shut?
SERVANTS. Yes.

---

[26]Swiss.
[27]An ornamented flap concealing the opening in the breeches.

ANTONIO. 'Tis the duchess's pleasure
  Each officer be locked into his chamber
  Till the sun-rising; and to send the keys
  Of all their chests and of their outward doors
  Into her bed-chamber. She is very sick.
RODERIGO. At her pleasure.
ANTONIO. She entreats you take 't not ill: the innocent
  Shall be the more approved by it.
BOSOLA. Gentlemen o' the wood-yard, where's your Switzer now?
1ST SERVANT. By this hand, 'twas credibly reported by one o' the
  blackguard.

  Exeunt all except ANTONIO *and* DELIO.

DELIO. How fares it with the duchess?
ANTONIO. She's exposed
  Unto the worst of torture, pain and fear.
DELIO. Speak to her all happy comfort.
ANTONIO. How I do play the fool with mine own danger!
  You are this night, dear friend, to post to Rome:
  My life lies in your service.
DELIO. Do not doubt me.
ANTONIO. O, 'tis far from me: and yet fear presents me
  Somewhat that looks like danger.
DELIO. Believe it,
  'Tis but the shadow of your fear, no more:
  How superstitiously we mind our evils!
  The throwing down salt, or crossing of a hare,
  Bleeding at nose, the stumbling of a horse,
  Or singing of a cricket, are of power
  To daunt whole man in us. Sir, fare you well:
  I wish you all the joys of a blessed father:
  And, for my faith, lay this unto your breast,—
  Old friends, like old swords, still are trusted best.   [*Exit*

  Enter CARIOLA.

CARIOLA. Sir, you are the happy father of a son:
  Your wife commends him to you.
ANTONIO. Blessed comfort!—
  For Heaven's sake tend her well: I'll presently
  Go set a figure for 's nativity.[28]   [*Exeunt*

---

[28]Cast a horoscope for the newborn baby.

Scene III

The court of the same palace.

Enter BOSOLA, *with a dark lantern.*

BOSOLA. Sure I did hear a woman shriek: list, ha!
    And the sound came, if I received it right,
    From the duchess's lodgings. There's some stratagem
    In the confining all our courtiers
    To their several wards: I must have part of it;
    My intelligence will freeze else. List, again!
    It may be 'twas the melancholy bird,
    Best friend of silence and of solitariness,
    The owl, that screamed so.—Ha! Antonio!

Enter ANTONIO.

ANTONIO. I heard some noise.—Who's there? what art thou? speak.
BOSOLA. Antonio, put not your face nor body
    To such a forced expression of fear:
    I am Bosola, your friend.
ANTONIO. Bosola!
    [*Aside*] This mole does undermine me.—Heard you not
    A noise even now?
BOSOLA. From whence?
ANTONIO. From the duchess's lodging.
BOSOLA. Not I: did you?
ANTONIO. I did, or else I dreamed.
BOSOLA. Let's walk towards it.
ANTONIO. No: it may be 'twas
    But the rising of the wind.
BOSOLA. Very likely.
    Methinks 'tis very cold, and yet you sweat:
    You look wildly.
ANTONIO. I have been setting a figure
    For the duchess's jewels.
BOSOLA. Ah, and how falls your question?
    Do you find it radical?[29]
ANTONIO. What's that to you?
    'Tis rather to be questioned what design,
    When all men were commanded to their lodgings,

---

[29]Fit to be judged.

Makes you a night-walker.

BOSOLA. In sooth, I'll tell you:
Now all the court's asleep, I thought the devil
Had least to do here; I came to say my prayers;
And if it do offend you I do so,
You are a fine courtier.

ANTONIO. [*Aside*] This fellow will undo me.—
You gave the duchess apricocks to-day:
Pray Heaven they were not poisoned!

BOSOLA. Poisoned! A Spanish fig
For the imputation.

ANTONIO. Traitors are ever confident
Till they are discovered. There were jewels stol'n too:
In my conceit, none are to be suspected
More than yourself.

BOSOLA. You are a false steward.

ANTONIO. Saucy slave, I'll pull thee up by the roots.

BOSOLA. May be the ruin will crush you to pieces.

ANTONIO. You are an impudent snake indeed, sir:
Are you scarce warm, and do you show your sting?
You libel well, sir.

BOSOLA. No, sir: copy it out,
And I will set my hand to 't.

ANTONIO. [*Aside*] My nose bleeds.
One that were superstitious would count
This ominous, when it merely comes by chance:
Two letters, that are wrote here for my name,
Are drowned in blood!
Mere accident.—For you, sir, I'll take order
I' the morn you shall be safe:—[*Aside*] 'tis that must color
Her lying-in:—sir, this door you pass not:
I do not hold it fit that you come near
The duchess's lodgings, till you have quit yourself.—
[*Aside*] The great are like the base, nay, they are the same,
When they seek shameful ways to avoid shame.   [*Exit*

BOSOLA. Antonio hereabout did drop a paper:—
Some of your help, false friend:—O, here it is.
What's here? a child's nativity calculated! [*Reads*]
"The duchess was delivered of a son, 'tween the hours twelve and
one in the night, *Anno Dom.* 1504,"—that's this year—"*decimo non
Decembris*,"—that's this night,—"taken according to the meridian of
Malfi,"—that's our duchess: happy discovery!—"The lord of the first
house being combust in the ascendant, signifies short life; and Mars

being in a human sign, joined to the tail of the Dragon, in the eighth
house, doth threaten a <u>violent death</u>. *Cœtera non scrutantur*."[30]
Why, now 'tis most apparent: this precise fellow
Is the duchess's bawd:[31]—I have it to my wish!
This is a parcel of intelligency
Our courtiers were cased up for: it needs must follow
That I must be committed on pretence
Of poisoning her; which I'll endure, and laugh at.
If one could find the father now! but that
Time will discover. Old Castruccio
I' the morning posts to Rome: by him I'll send
A letter that shall make her brothers' galls
O'erflow their livers. This was a thrifty way.
Though lust do mask in ne'er so strange disguise,
She's oft found witty, but is never wise.   [*Exit*

Scene IV

An apartment in the palace of the CARDINAL *at Rome.*

Enter CARDINAL *and* JULIA.

CARDINAL. Sit: thou art my best of wishes. Prithee, tell me
    What trick didst thou invent to come to Rome
    Without thy husband.
JULIA. Why, my lord, I told him
    I came to visit an old anchorite
    Here for devotion.
CARDINAL. Thou art a witty false one,—
    I mean, to him.
JULIA. You have prevailed with me
    Beyond my strongest thoughts: I would not now
    Find you inconstant.
CARDINAL. Do not put yourself
    To such a voluntary torture, which proceeds
    Out of your own guilt.
JULIA. How, my lord!
CARDINAL. You fear
    My constancy, because you have approved
    Those giddy and wild turnings in yourself.

---

[30]The rest is not investigated.
[31]Pander.

JULIA. Did you e'er find them?
CARDINAL. Sooth, generally for women,
  A man might strive to make glass malleable,
  Ere he should make them fixèd.
JULIA. So, my lord.
CARDINAL. We had need go borrow that fantastic glass
  Invented by Galileo the Florentine
  To view another spacious world i' the moon,
  And look to find a constant woman there.
JULIA. This is very well, my lord.
CARDINAL. Why do you weep?
  Are tears your justification? the self-same tears
  Will fall into your husband's bosom, lady,
  With a loud protestation that you love him
  Above the world. Come, I'll love you wisely,
  That's jealousy; since I am very certain
  You cannot make me cuckold.
JULIA. I'll go home
  To my husband.
CARDINAL. You may thank me, lady,
  I have taken you off your melancholy perch,
  Bore you upon my fist, and showed you game,
  And let you fly at it.—I pray thee, kiss me.—
  When thou wast with thy husband, thou wast watched
  Like a tame elephant:—still you are to thank me:—
  Thou hadst only kisses from him and high feeding;
  But what delight was that? 'twas just like one
  That hath a little fingering on the lute,
  Yet cannot tune it:—still you are to thank me.
JULIA. You told me of a piteous wound i' the heart ·
  And a sick liver, when you wooed me first,
  And spake like one in physic.
CARDINAL. Who's that?—

Enter SERVANT.

  Rest firm, for my affection to thee,
  Lightning moves slow to 't.
SERVANT. Madam, a gentleman,
  That's come post from Malfi, desires to see you.
CARDINAL. Let him enter: I'll withdraw.   [*Exit*
SERVANT. He says
  Your husband, old Castruccio, is come to Rome,
  Most pitifully tired with riding post.   [*Exit*

Enter DELIO.

JULIA. [*Aside*] Signior Delio! 'tis one of my old suitors.
DELIO. I was bold to come and see you.
JULIA. Sir, you are welcome.
DELIO. Do you lie here?
JULIA. Sure, your own experience
    Will satisfy you no: our Roman prelates
    Do not keep lodging for ladies.
DELIO. Very well:
    I have brought you no commendations from your husband,
    For I know none by him.
JULIA. I hear he's come to Rome.
DELIO. I never knew man and beast, of a horse and a knight,
    So weary of each other: if he had had a good back,
    He would have undertook to have borne his horse,
    His breech was so pitifully sore.
JULIA. Your laughter
    Is my pity.
DELIO. Lady, I know not whether
    You want money, but I have brought you some.
JULIA. From my husband?
DELIO. No, from mine own allowance.
JULIA. I must hear the condition, ere I be bound to take it.
DELIO. Look on 't, 'tis gold: hath it not a fine color?
JULIA. I have a bird more beautiful.
DELIO. Try the sound on 't.
JULIA. A lute-string far exceeds it:
    It hath no smell, like cassia or civet;
    Nor is it physical, though some fond doctors
    Persuade us seethe 't in cullises.[32] I'll tell you,
    This is a creature bred by—

Re-enter SERVANT.

SERVANT. Your husband's come,
    Hath delivered a letter to the Duke of Calabria
    That, to my thinking, hath put him out of his wits.   [*Exit*
JULIA. Sir, you hear:
    Pray, let me know your business and your suit
    As briefly as can be.

---

[32]Strong broths. The old recipe-books recommend "pieces of gold" among the
ingredients.

DELIO. With good speed: I would wish you,
  At such time as you are non-resident
  With your husband, my mistress.
JULIA. Sir, I'll go ask my husband if I shall,
  And straight return your answer.   [*Exit*
DELIO. Very fine!
  Is this her wit, or honesty, that speaks thus?
  I heard one say the duke was highly moved
  With a letter sent from Malfi. I do fear
  Antonio is betrayed: how fearfully
  Shows his ambition now! unfortunate fortune!
  They pass through whirlpools, and deep woes do shun,
  Who the event weigh ere the action's done.   [*Exit*

Scene V

Another apartment in the same palace.

Enter CARDINAL *and* FERDINAND *with a letter.*

FERDINAND. I have this night digged up a mandrake.
CARDINAL. Say you?
FERDINAND. And I am grown mad with 't.
CARDINAL. What's the prodigy?
FERDINAND. Read there,—a sister damned: she's loose i' the hilts;
  Grown a notorious strumpet.
CARDINAL. Speak lower.
FERDINAND. Lower!
  Rogues do not whisper 't now, but seek to publish 't
  (As servants do the bounty of their lords)
  Aloud; and with a covetous searching eye,
  To mark who note them. O, confusion seize her!
  She hath had most cunning bawds to serve her turn,
  And more secure conveyances for lust
  Than towns of garrison for service.
CARDINAL. Is 't possible?
  Can this be certain?
FERDINAND. Rhubarb, O, for rhubarb
  To purge this choler! here's the cursèd day
  To prompt my memory; and here 't shall stick
  Till of her bleeding heart I make a sponge
  To wipe it out.
CARDINAL. Why do you make yourself

So wild a tempest?
FERDINAND. Would I could be one,
  That I might toss her palace 'bout her ears,
  Root up her goodly forests, blast her meads,
  And lay her general territory as waste
  As she hath done her honors.
CARDINAL. Shall our blood,
  The royal blood of Aragon and Castile,
  Be thus attainted?
FERDINAND. Apply desperate physic:
  We must not now use balsamum, but fire,
  The smarting cupping-glass, for that's the mean
  To purge infected blood, such blood as hers.
  There is a kind of pity in mine eye,—
  I'll give it to my handkercher; and now 'tis here,
  I'll bequeath this to her bastard.
CARDINAL. What to do?
FERDINAND. Why, to make soft lint for his mother's wounds,
  When I have hewed her to pieces.
CARDINAL. Cursèd creature!
  Unequal nature, to place women's hearts
  So far upon the left side!
FERDINAND. Foolish men,
  That e'er will trust their honor in a bark
  Made of so slight weak bulrush as is woman,
  Apt every minute to sink it!
CARDINAL. Thus
  Ignorance, when it hath purchased honor,
  It cannot wield it.
FERDINAND. Methinks I see her laughing—
  Excellent hyena! Talk to me somewhat quickly,
  Or my imagination will carry me
  To see her in the shameful act of sin.
CARDINAL. With whom?
FERDINAND. Happily with some strong-thighed bargeman,
  Or one o' the woodyard that can quoit the sledge
  Or toss the bar, or else some lovely squire
  That carries coals up to her privy lodgings.
CARDINAL. You fly beyond your reason.
FERDINAND. Go to, mistress!
  'Tis not your whore's milk that shall quench my wild fire,
  But your whore's blood.
CARDINAL. How idly shows this rage, which carries you,

As men conveyed by witches through the air,
On violent whirlwinds! this intemperate noise
Fitly resembles deaf men's shrill discourse,
Who talk aloud, thinking all other men
To have their imperfection.
FERDINAND. Have not you
  My palsy?
CARDINAL. Yes, but I can be angry
  Without this rupture: there is not in nature
  A thing that makes man so deformed, so beastly,
  As doth intemperate anger. Chide yourself.
  You have divers men who never yet expressed
  Their strong desire of rest but by unrest,
  By vexing of themselves. Come, put yourself
  In tune.
FERDINAND. So I will only study to seem
  The thing I am not. I could kill her now,
  In you, or in myself; for I do think
  It is some sin in us Heaven doth revenge
  By her.
CARDINAL. Are you stark mad?
FERDINAND. I would have their bodies
  Burnt in a coal-pit with the ventage stopped,
  That their cursed smoke might not ascend to Heaven
  Or dip the sheets they lie in in pitch or sulphur,
  Wrap them in 't, and then light them like a match;
  Or else to boil their bastard to a cullis,
  And give 't his lecherous father to renew
  The sin of his back.
CARDINAL. I'll leave you.
FERDINAND. Nay, I have done.
  I am confident, had I been damned in hell,
  And should have heard of this, it would have put me
  Into a cold sweat. In, in; I'll go sleep.
  Till I know who leaps my sister, I'll not stir:
  That known, I'll find scorpions to string my whips,
  And fix her in a general eclipse.   [*Exeunt*

ACT III

Scene I

An apartment in the palace of the DUCHESS.

Enter ANTONIO *and* DELIO.

ANTONIO. Our noble friend, my most belovèd Delio!
  O, you have been a stranger long at court;
  Came you along with the Lord Ferdinand?
DELIO. I did, sir. and how fares your noble duchess?
ANTONIO. Right fortunately well: she's an excellent
  Feeder of pedigrees; since you last saw her,
  She hath had two children more, a son and daughter.
DELIO. Methinks 'twas yesterday: let me but wink,
  And not behold your face, which to mine eye
  Is somewhat leaner, verily I should dream
  It were within this half hour.
ANTONIO. You have not been in law, friend Delio,
  Nor in prison, nor a suitor at the court,
  Nor begged the reversion of some great man's place,
  Nor troubled with an old wife, which doth make
  Your time so insensibly hasten.
DELIO. Pray, sir, tell me,
  Hath not this news arrived yet to the ear
  Of the lord cardinal?
ANTONIO. I fear it hath:
  The Lord Ferdinand, that's newly come to court,
  Doth bear himself right dangerously.
DELIO. Pray, why?
ANTONIO. He is so quiet that he seems to sleep
  The tempest out, as dormice do in winter:

33

Those houses that are haunted are most still
Till the devil be up.
DELIO. What say the common people?
ANTONIO. The common rabble do directly say
She is a strumpet.
DELIO. And your graver heads
Which would be politic, what censure they?
ANTONIO. They do observe I grow to infinite purchase,
The left hand way, and all suppose the duchess
Would amend it, if she could; for, say they,
Great princes, though they grudge their officers
Should have such large and unconfinèd means
To get wealth under them, will not complain,
Lest thereby they should make them odious
Unto the people; for other obligation
Of love or marriage between her and me
They never dream of.
DELIO. The Lord Ferdinand
Is going to bed.

Enter DUCHESS, FERDINAND, *and* ATTENDANTS.

FERDINAND. I'll instantly to bed,
For I am weary.—I am to bespeak
A husband for you.
DUCHESS. For me, sir! pray, who is 't?
FERDINAND. The great Count Malatesti.
DUCHESS. Fie upon him!
A count! he's a mere stick of sugar-candy;
You may look quite through him. When I choose
A husband, I will marry for your honor.
FERDINAND. You shall do well in 't.—How is 't, worthy Antonio?
DUCHESS. But, sir, I am to have private conference with you
About a scandalous report is spread
Touching mine honor.
FERDINAND. Let me be ever deaf to 't:
One of Pasquil's paper bullets,[33] court-calumny,
A pestilent air, which princes' palaces
Are seldom purged of. Yet say that it were true,
I pour it in your bosom, my fixed love
Would strongly excuse, extenuate, nay, deny
Faults, were they apparent in you. Go, be safe

---

[33]Scurrilous verses.

In your own innocency.
DUCHESS. [*Aside*] O blessed comfort!
This deadly air is purged.

Exeunt DUCHESS, ANTONIO, DELIO, *and* ATTENDANTS.

FERDINAND. Her guilt treads on
Hot-burning coulters.

Enter BOSOLA.

Now, Bosola,
How thrives our intelligence?
BOSOLA. Sir, uncertainly:
'Tis rumored she hath had three bastards, but
By whom we may go read i' the stars.
FERDINAND. Why, some
Hold opinion all things are written there.
BOSOLA. Yes, if we could find spectacles to read them.
I do suspect there hath been some sorcery
Used on the duchess.
FERDINAND. Sorcery! to what purpose?
BOSOLA. To make her dote on some desertless fellow
She shames to acknowledge.
FERDINAND. Can your faith give way
To think there's power in potions or in charms,
To make us love whether we will or no?
BOSOLA. Most certainly.
FERDINAND. Away! these are mere gulleries, horrid things,
Invented by some cheating mountebanks
To abuse us. Do you think that herbs or charms
Can force the will? Some trials have been made
In this foolish practice, but the ingredients
Were lenitive poisons, such as are of force
To make the patient mad; and straight the witch
Swears by equivocation they are in love.
The witchcraft lies in her rank blood. This night
I will force confession from her. You told me
You had got, within these two days, a false key
Into her bed-chamber.
BOSOLA. I have.
FERDINAND. As I would wish.
BOSOLA. What do you intend to do?
FERDINAND. Can you guess?
BOSOLA. No.

FERDINAND. Do not ask, then:
  He that can compass me, and know my drifts,
  May say he hath put a girdle 'bout the world,
  And sounded all her quicksands.
BOSOLA. I do not
  Think so.
FERDINAND. What do you think, then, pray?
BOSOLA. That you are
  Your own chronicle too much, and grossly
  Flatter yourself.
FERDINAND. Give me thy hand; I thank thee:
  I never gave pension but to flatterers,
  Till I entertainèd thee. Farewell.
  That friend a great man's ruin strongly checks,
  Who rails into his belief all his defects.   [*Exeunt*

Scene II

The bed-chamber of the DUCHESS.

Enter DUCHESS, ANTONIO, *and* CARIOLA.

DUCHESS. Bring me the casket hither, and the glass.—You get no lodg-
  ing here tonight, my lord.
ANTONIO. Indeed, I must persuade one.
DUCHESS. Very good:
  I hope in time 'twill grow into a custom,
  That noblemen shall come with cap and knee
  To purchase a night's lodging of their wives.
ANTONIO. I must lie here.
DUCHESS. Must! you are a lord of misrule.
ANTONIO. Indeed, my rule is only in the night.
DUCHESS. To what use will you put me?
ANTONIO. We'll sleep together.
DUCHESS. Alas,
  What pleasure can two lovers find in sleep!
CARIOLA. My lord, I lie with her often; and I know
  She'll much disquiet you.
ANTONIO. See, you are complained of.
CARIOLA. For she's the sprawling'st bedfellow.
ANTONIO. I shall like her the better for that.
CARIOLA. Sir, shall I ask you a question?
ANTONIO. Ay, pray thee, Cariola.

CARIOLA. Wherefore still, when you lie with my lady,
  Do you rise so early?
ANTONIO. Laboring men
  Count the clock oftenest, Cariola,
  Are glad when their task's ended.
DUCHESS. I'll stop your mouth. *—whoh-forward!*   [*Kisses him*
ANTONIO. Nay, that's but one; Venus had two soft doves
  To draw her chariot; I must have another—   [*She kisses him again*
  When wilt thou marry, Cariola?
CARIOLA. Never, my lord.
ANTONIO. O, fie upon this single life! forego it.
  We read how Daphne, for her peevish flight,
  Became a fruitless bay-tree; Syrinx turned
  To the pale empty reed; Anaxarete
  Was frozen into marble: whereas those
  Which married, or proved kind unto their friends,
  Were by a gracious influence transhaped
  Into the olive, pomegranate, mulberry,
  Became flowers, precious stones, or eminent stars.
CARIOLA. This is a vain poetry: but I pray you tell me,
  If there were proposed me, wisdom, riches, and beauty,
  In three several young men, which should I choose.
ANTONIO. 'Tis a hard question: this was Paris's case,
  And he was blind in 't, and there was great cause;
  For how was 't possible he could judge right,
  Having three amorous goddesses in view,
  And they stark naked? 'twas a motion
  Were able to benight the apprehension
  Of the severest counsellor of Europe.
  Now I look on both your faces so well formed,
  It puts me in mind of a question I would ask.
CARIOLA. What is 't?
ANTONIO. I do wonder why hard-favored ladies,
  For the most part, keep worse-favored waiting-women
  To attend them, and cannot endure fair ones.
DUCHESS. O, that's soon answered.
  Did you ever in your life know an ill painter
  Desire to have his dwelling next door to the shop
  Of an excellent picture-maker? 'twould disgrace
  His face-making, and undo him. I prithee,
  When were we so merry?—My hair tangles.
ANTONIO. Pray thee, Cariola, let's steal forth the room,
  And let her talk to herself: I have divers times

Served her the like, when she hath chafed extremely.
I love to see her angry. Softly, Cariola.

Exeunt ANTONIO *and* CARIOLA.

DUCHESS. Doth not the color of my hair 'gin to change?
When I wax gray, I shall have all the court
Powder their hair with arras,[34] to be like me.
You have cause to love me; I entered you into my heart
Before you would vouchsafe to call for the keys.

Enter FERDINAND *behind*.

We shall one day have my brothers take you napping;
Methinks his presence, being now in court,
Should make you keep your own bed; but you'll say
Love mixed with fear is sweetest. I'll assure you,
You shall get no more children till my brothers
Consent to be your gossips.[35] Have you lost your tongue?
'Tis welcome:
For know, whether I am doomed to live or die,
I can do both like a prince.
FERDINAND. Die, then, quickly!   [*Giving her a poniard*
Virtue, where art thou hid? what hideous thing
Is it that doth eclipse thee?
DUCHESS. Pray, sir, hear me.
FERDINAND. Or is it true thou art but a bare name,
And no essential thing?
DUCHESS. Sir,—
FERDINAND. Do not speak.
DUCHESS. No, sir:
I will plant my soul in mine ears, to hear you.
FERDINAND. O most imperfect light of human reason,
That mak'st us so unhappy to foresee
What we can least prevent! Pursue thy wishes,
And glory in them: there's in shame no comfort
But to be past all bounds and sense of shame.
DUCHESS. I pray, sir, hear me: I am married.
FERDINAND. So!
DUCHESS. Happily, not to your liking: but for that,
Alas, your shears do come untimely now
To clip the bird's wing that's already flown!

---

[34]Orrisroot, the rootstock of irises, used in perfumes.
[35]Godparents.

Will you see my husband?
FERDINAND. Yes, if I could change
Eyes with a basilisk.
DUCHESS. Sure, you came hither
By his confederacy.
FERDINAND. The howling of a wolf
Is music to thee, screech-owl: prithee, peace.—
Whate'er thou art that hast enjoyed my sister,
For I am sure thou hear'st me, for thine own sake
Let me not know thee. I came hither prepared
To work thy discovery; yet am now persuaded
It would beget such violent effects
As would damn us both. I would not for ten millions
I had beheld thee: therefore use all means
I never may have knowledge of thy name;
Enjoy thy lust still, and a wretched life,
On that condition.—And for thee, vile woman,
If thou do wish thy lecher may grow old
In thy embracements, I would have thee build
Such a room for him as our anchorites
To holier use inhabit. Let not the sun
Shine on him till he's dead; let dogs and monkeys
Only converse with him, and such dumb things
To whom nature denies use to sound his name;
Do not keep a paraquito, lest she learn it;
If thou do love him, cut out thine own tongue,
Lest it bewray him.
DUCHESS. Why might not I marry?
I have not gone about in this to create
Any new world or custom.
FERDINAND. Thou art undone;
And thou hast ta'en that massy sheet of lead
That hid thy husband's bones, and folded it
About my heart.
DUCHESS. Mine bleeds for 't.
FERDINAND. Thine! thy heart!
What should I name 't unless a hollow bullet
Filled with unquenchable wild-fire?
DUCHESS. You are in this
Too strict; and were you not my princely brother,
I would say, too wilful: my reputation
Is safe.
FERDINAND. Dost thou know what reputation is?

I'll tell thee,—to small purpose, since the instruction
Comes now too late.
Upon a time Reputation, Love, and Death,
Would travel o'er the world; and it was concluded
That they should part, and take three several ways.
Death told them, they should find him in great battles,
Or cities plagued with plagues: Love gives them counsel
To inquire for him 'mongst unambitious shepherds,
Where dowries were not talked of, and sometimes
'Mongst quiet kindred that had nothing left
By their dead parents: "Stay," quoth Reputation,
"Do not forsake me; for it is my nature,
If once I part from any man I meet,
I am never found again." And so for you:
You have shook hands with Reputation,
And made him invisible. So, fare you well:
I will never see you more.

DUCHESS. Why should only I,
Of all the other princes of the world,
Be cased up, like a holy relic? I have youth
And a little beauty.

FERDINAND. So you have some virgins
That are witches. I will never see thee more.   [*Exit*

Re-enter ANTONIO *with a pistol, and* CARIOLA.

DUCHESS. You saw this apparition?

ANTONIO. Yes: we are
Betrayed. How came he hither? I should turn
This to thee, for that.

CARIOLA. Pray, sir, do; and when
That you have cleft my heart, you shall read there
Mine innocence.

DUCHESS. That gallery gave him entrance.

ANTONIO. I would this terrible thing would come again,
That, standing on my guard, I might relate
My warrantable love.—

She shows the poniard.

Ha! what means this?

DUCHESS. He left this with me.

ANTONIO. And it seems did wish
You would use it on yourself.

DUCHESS. His action

Seemed to intend so much.
ANTONIO. This hath a handle to 't,
As well as a point: turn it towards him,
And so fasten the keen edge in his rank gall.

Knocking within.

How now! who knocks? more earthquakes?
DUCHESS. I stand
As if a mine beneath my feet were ready
To be blown up.
CARIOLA. 'Tis Bosola.
DUCHESS. Away!
O misery! methinks unjust actions
Should wear these masks and curtains, and not we.
You must instantly part hence: I have fashioned it already.

Exit ANTONIO. *Enter* BOSOLA.

BOSOLA. The duke your brother is ta'en up in a whirlwind;
Hath took horse, and 's rid post to Rome.
DUCHESS. So late?
BOSOLA. He told me, as he mounted into the saddle,
You were undone.
DUCHESS. Indeed, I am very near it.
BOSOLA. What's the matter?
DUCHESS. Antonio, the master of our household,
Hath dealt so falsely with me in 's accounts:
My brother stood engaged with me for money
Ta'en up of certain Neapolitan Jews,
And Antonio lets the bonds be forfeit.
BOSOLA. Strange!—[*Aside*] This is cunning.
DUCHESS. And hereupon
My brother's bills at Naples are protested
Against.—Call up our officers.
BOSOLA. I shall.   [*Exit*

Re-enter ANTONIO.

DUCHESS. The place that you must fly to is Ancona:
Hire a house there; I'll send after you
My treasure and my jewels. Our weak safety
Runs upon enginous[36] wheels: short syllables
Must stand for periods. I must now accuse you

---

[36]Rapid.

Of such a feignèd crime as Tasso calls
Magnanima menzogna, a noble lie,
'Cause it must shield our honors.—Hark! they are coming.

Re-enter BOSOLA *and* OFFICERS.

ANTONIO. Will your grace hear me?
DUCHESS. I have got well by you; you have yielded me
A million of loss: I am like to inherit
The people's curses for your stewardship.
You had the trick in audit-time to be sick,
Till I had signed your quietus;[37] and that cured you
Without help of a doctor.—Gentlemen,
I would have this man be an example to you all;
So shall you hold my favor; I pray, let him;
For he's done that, alas, you would not think of,
And, because I intend to be rid of him,
I mean not to publish.—Use your fortune elsewhere.
ANTONIO. I am strongly armed to brook my overthrow,
As commonly men bear with a hard year:
I will not blame the cause on 't; but do think
The necessity of my malevolent star
Procures this, not her humor. O, the inconstant
And rotten ground of service! you may see,
'Tis even like him, that in a winter night,
Takes a long slumber o'er a dying fire,
As loth to part from 't; yet parts thence as cold
As when he first sat down.
DUCHESS. We do confiscate,
Towards the satisfying of your accounts,
All that you have.
ANTONIO. I am all yours; and 'tis very fit
All mine should be so.
DUCHESS. So, sir, you have your pass.
ANTONIO. You may see, gentlemen, what 'tis to serve
A prince with body and soul. [*Exit*
BOSOLA. Here's an example for extortion: what moisture is drawn out of
the sea, when foul weather comes, pours down, and runs into the sea
again.
DUCHESS. I would know what are your opinions
Of this Antonio.

---

[37]Here, death certificate; *Quietus* was used playfully in Act I, Scene I.

2ND OFFICER. He could not abide to see a pig's head gaping: I thought your grace would find him a Jew.

3RD OFFICER. I would you had been his officer, for your own sake.

4TH OFFICER. You would have had more money.

1ST OFFICER. He stopped his ears with black wool, and to those came to him for money said he was thick of hearing.

2ND OFFICER. Some said he was an hermaphrodite, for he could not abide a woman.

4TH OFFICER. How scurvy proud he would look when the treasury was full! Well, let him go.

1ST OFFICER. Yes, and the chippings of the butterfly after him, to scour his gold chain.

DUCHESS. Leave us.

Exeunt OFFICERS.

What do you think of these?

BOSOLA. That these are rogues that in 's prosperity,
But to have waited on his fortune, could have wished
His dirty stirrup rivetted through their noses,
And followed after 's mule, like a bear in a ring;
Would have prostituted their daughters to his lust;
Made their first-born intelligencers; thought none happy
But such as were born under his blest planet,
And wore his livery: and do these lice drop off now?
Well, never look to have the like again:
He hath left a sort of flattering rogues behind him;
Their doom must follow. Princes pay flatterers
In their own money: flatterers dissemble their vices,
And they dissemble their lies; that's justice.
Alas, poor gentleman!

DUCHESS. Poor! he hath amply filled his coffers.

BOSOLA. Sure, he was too honest. Pluto, the god of riches,
When he's sent by Jupiter to any man,
He goes limping, to signify that wealth
That comes on God's name comes slowly; but when he's sent
On the devil's errand, he rides post and comes in by scuttles.[38]
Let me show you what a most unvalued jewel
You have in a wanton humor thrown away,
To bless the man shall find him. He was an excellent
Courtier and most faithful; a soldier that thought it

---

[38]A quick run.

As beastly to know his own value too little
As devilish to acknowledge it too much.
Both his virtue and form deserved a far better fortune:
His discourse rather delighted to judge itself than show itself:
His breast was filled with all perfection,
And yet it seemed a private whispering-room,
It made so little noise of 't.
DUCHESS. But he was basely descended.
BOSOLA. Will you make yourself a mercenary herald,
Rather to examine men's pedigrees than virtues?
You shall want him:
For know an honest statesman to a prince
Is like a cedar planted by a spring;
The spring bathes the tree's root, the grateful tree
Rewards it with his shadow: you have not done so.
I would sooner swim to the Bermoothes[39] on
Two politicians' rotten bladders, tied
Together with an intelligencer's heartstring,
Than depend on so changeable a prince's favor.
Fare thee well, Antonio! since the malice of the world
Would needs down with thee, it cannot be said yet
That any ill happened unto thee, considering thy fall
Was accompanied with virtue.
DUCHESS. O, you render me excellent music!
BOSOLA. Say you?
DUCHESS. This good one that you speak of is my husband.
BOSOLA. Do I not dream! can this ambitious age
Have so much goodness in 't as to prefer
A man merely for worth, without these shadows
Of wealth and painted honors? possible?
DUCHESS. I have had three children by him.
BOSOLA. Fortunate lady!
For you have made your private nuptial bed
The humble and fair seminary of peace.
No question but many an unbeneficed scholar
Shall pray for you for this deed, and rejoice
That some preferment in the world can yet
Arise from merit. The virgins of your land
That have no dowries shall hope your example
Will raise them to rich husbands. Should you want

---

[39]Bermudas.

Soldiers, 'twould make the very Turks and Moors
Turn Christians, and serve you for this act.
Last, the neglected poets of your time,
In honor of this trophy of a man,
Raised by that curious engine, your white hand,
Shall thank you, in your grave, for 't; and make that
More reverend than all the cabinets
Of living princes. For Antonio.
His fame shall likewise flow from many a pen,
When heralds shall want coats to sell to men.

DUCHESS. As I taste comfort in this friendly speech,
So would I find concealment.

BOSOLA. O, the secret of my prince,
Which I will wear on the inside of my heart!

DUCHESS. You shall take charge of all my coin and jewels
And follow him; for he retires himself
To Ancona.

BOSOLA. So.

DUCHESS. Whither, within few days,
I mean to follow thee.

BOSOLA. Let me think:
I would wish your grace to feign a pilgrimage
To our Lady of Loretto, scarce seven leagues
From fair Ancona; so may you depart
Your country with more honor, and your flight
Will seem a princely progress, retaining
Your usual train about you.

DUCHESS. Sir, your direction
Shall lead me by the hand.

CARIOLA. In my opinion,
She were better progress to the baths at Lucca,
Or go visit the Spa
In Germany; for, if you will believe me,
I do not like this jesting with religion,
This feignèd pilgrimage.

DUCHESS. Thou art a superstitious fool:
Prepare us instantly for our departure.
Past sorrows, let us moderately lament them;
For those to come, seek wisely to prevent them.

Exeunt DUCHESS *and* CARIOLA.

BOSOLA. A politician is the devil's quilted anvil;
He fashions all sins on him, and the blows

Are never heard: he may work in a lady's chamber,
As here for proof. What rests but I reveal
All to my lord? O, this base quality
Of intelligencer! why, every quality i' the world
Prefers but gain or commendation:
Now for this act I am certain to be raised,
And men that paint weeds to the life are praised.   [*Exit*

Scene III

An apartment in the CARDINAL'*s palace at Rome.*

Enter CARDINAL, FERDINAND, MALATESTI, PESCARA, DELIO, *and*
SILVIO.

CARDINAL. Must we turn soldier, then?
MALATESTI. The emperor,
    Hearing your worth that way, ere you attained
    This reverend garment, joins you in commission
    With the right fortunate soldier the Marquis of Pescara,
    And the famous Lannoy.
CARDINAL. He that had the honor
    Of taking the French king prisoner?
MALATESTI. The same.
    Here's a plot drawn for a new fortification
    At Naples.
FERDINAND. This great Count Malatesti, I perceive,
    Hath got employment?
DELIO. No employment, my lord;
    A marginal note in the muster-book, that he is
    A voluntary lord.
FERDINAND. He's no soldier.
DELIO. He has worn gunpowder in 's hollow tooth for the toothache.
SILVIO. He comes to the leaguer[40] with a full intent
    To eat fresh beef and garlic, means to stay
    Till the scent be gone, and straight return to court.
DELIO. He hath read all the late service
    As the city chronicle relates it;
    And keeps two pewterers going, only to express
    Battles in model.
SILVIO. Then he'll fight by the book.

---

[40]Camp.

DELIO. By the almanac, I think,
To choose good days and shun the critical;
That's his mistress's scarf.
SILVIO. Yes, he protests
He would do much for that taffeta.
DELIO. I think he would run away from a battle,
To save it from taking prisoner.
SILVIO. He is horribly afraid
Gunpowder will spoil the perfume on 't.
DELIO. I saw a Dutchman break his pate once
For calling him pot-gun; he made his head
Have a bore in 't like a musket.
SILVIO. I would he had made a touchhole to 't.
He is indeed a guarded sumpter-cloth,
Only for the remove of the court.

Enter BOSOLA.

PESCARA. Bosola arrived! what should be the business?
Some falling-out amongst the cardinals.
These factions amongst great men, they are like
Foxes, when their heads are divided,
They carry fire in their tails, and all the country
About them goes to wreck for 't.
SILVIO. What's that Bosola?
DELIO. I knew him in Padua a fantastical scholar, like such who
study to know how many knots was in Hercules' club, of what color
Achilles' beard was, or whether Hector were not troubled with the
toothache. He hath studied himself half blear-eyed to know the true
symmetry of Cæsar's nose by a shoeing-horn; and this he did to gain
the name of a speculative man.
PESCARA. Mark Prince Ferdinand:
A very salamander lives in 's eye,
To mock the eager violence of fire.
SILVIO. That cardinal hath made more bad faces with his oppression
than ever Michael Angelo made good ones: he lifts up 's nose, like a
foul porpoise before a storm.
PESCARA. The Lord Ferdinand laughs.
DELIO. Like a deadly cannon
That lightens ere it smokes.
PESCARA. These are your true pangs of death,
The pangs of life, that struggle with great statesmen.
DELIO. In such a deformed silence witches whisper their charms.
CARDINAL. Doth she make religion her riding-hood

To keep her from the sun and tempest?
FERDINAND. That,
  That damns her. Methinks her fault and beauty,
  Blended together, show like leprosy,
  The whiter, the fouler. I make it a question
  Whether her beggarly brats were ever christened.
CARDINAL. I will instantly solicit the state of Ancona
  To have them banished.
FERDINAND. You are for Loretto:
  I shall not be at your ceremony; fare you well.—
  Write to the Duke of Malfi, my young nephew
  She had by her first husband, and acquaint him
  With 's mother's honesty.
BOSOLA. I will.
FERDINAND. Antonio!
  A slave that only smelled of ink and counters,
  And never in 's life looked like a gentleman,
  But in the audit-time.—Go, go presently,
  Draw me out an hundred and fifty of our horse,
  And meet me at the fort-bridge.   [*Exeunt*

Scene IV

The shrine of Our Lady of Loretto.

Enter TWO PILGRIMS.

1ST PILGRIM. I have not seen a goodlier shrine than this;
  Yet I have visited many.
2ND PILGRIM. The Cardinal of Aragon
  Is this day to resign his cardinal's hat:
  His sister duchess likewise is arrived
  To pay her vow of pilgrimage. I expect
  A noble ceremony.
1ST PILGRIM. No question.—They come.

Here the ceremony of the CARDINAL's *instalment, in the habit of a soldier, is performed by his delivering up his cross, hat, robes, and ring, at the shrine, and the investing of him with sword, helmet, shield, and spurs; then* ANTONIO, *the* DUCHESS, *and the* CHILDREN, *having presented themselves at the shrine, are, by a form of banishment in dumbshow expressed towards them by the* CARDINAL *and the state of Ancona, banished: during all which ceremony, this ditty is sung, to very solemn music, by divers churchmen.*

Arms and honors deck thy story,
To thy fame's eternal glory!
Adverse fortune ever fly thee;
No disastrous fate come nigh thee!
I alone will sing thy praises,
Whom to honor virtue raises;
And thy study, that divine is,
Bent to martial discipline is.
Lay aside all those robes lie by thee;
Crown thy arts with arms, they'll beautify thee.
O worthy of worthiest name, adorned in this manner,
Lead bravely thy forces on under war's warlike banner!
O, mayst thou prove fortunate in all martial courses!
Guide thou still by skill in arts and forces!
Victory attend thee nigh, whilst fame sings loud thy powers;
Triumphant conquest crown thy head, and blessings pour down
showers!

Exeunt all except the TWO PILGRIMS.

1ST PILGRIM. Here's a strange turn of state! who would have thought
So great a lady would have matched herself
Unto so mean a person? yet the cardinal
Bears himself much too cruel.
2ND PILGRIM. They are banished.
1ST PILGRIM. But I would ask what power hath this state
Of Ancona to determine of a free prince?
2ND PILGRIM. They are a free state, sir, and her brother showed
How that the Pope, fore-hearing of her looseness,
Hath seized into the protection of the church
The dukedom which she held as dowager.
1ST PILGRIM. But by what justice?
2ND PILGRIM. Sure, I think by none,
Only her brother's instigation.
1ST PILGRIM. What was it with such violence he took
Off from her finger?
2ND PILGRIM. 'Twas her wedding-ring;
Which he vowed shortly he would sacrifice
To his revenge.
1ST PILGRIM. Alas, Antonio!
If that a man be thrust into a well,
No matter who sets hand to 't, his own weight
Will bring him sooner to the bottom. Come, let's hence.
Fortune makes this conclusion general,
All things do help the unhappy man to fall.   [*Exeunt*

Scene V

Near Loretto.

Enter DUCHESS, ANTONIO, CHILDREN, CARIOLA, *and* SERVANTS.

DUCHESS. Banished Ancona!
ANTONIO. Yes, you see what power
  Lightens in great men's breath.
DUCHESS. Is all our train
  Shrunk to this poor remainder?
ANTONIO. These poor men,
  Which have got little in your service, vow
  To take your fortune: but your wiser buntings,[41]
  Now they are fledged, are gone.
DUCHESS. They have done wisely.
  This puts me in mind of death: physicians thus,
  With their hands full of money, use to give o'er
  Their patients.
ANTONIO. Right the fashion of the world:
  From decayed fortunes every flatterer shrinks;
  Men cease to build where the foundation sinks.
DUCHESS. I had a very strange dream tonight.
ANTONIO. What was 't?
DUCHESS. Methought I wore my coronet of state,
  And on a sudden all the diamonds
  Were changed to pearls.
ANTONIO. My interpretation
  Is, you'll weep shortly; for to me the pearls
  Do signify your tears.
DUCHESS. The birds that live i' the field
  On the wild benefit of nature live
  Happier than we; for they may choose their mates,
  And carol their sweet pleasures to the spring.

Enter BOSOLA *with a letter.*

BOSOLA. You are happily o'erta'en.
DUCHESS. From my brother?
BOSOLA. Yes, from the Lord Ferdinand your brother
  All love and safety.
DUCHESS. Thou dost blanch mischief,
  Wouldst make it white. See, see, like to calm weather

---

[41]A bird that resembles a lark but does not possess its voice.

At sea before a tempest, false hearts speak fair
To those they intend most mischief.
[*Reads*] "Send Antonio to me; I want his head in a business."
A politic equivocation!
He doth not want your counsel, but your head;
That is, he cannot sleep till you be dead.
And here's another pitfall that's strewed o'er
With roses; mark it, 'tis a cunning one:
[*Reads*] "I stand engaged for your husband for several debts at
Naples: let not that trouble him; I had rather have his heart than his
money": —
And I believe so too.
BOSOLA. What do you believe?
DUCHESS. That he so much distrusts my husband's love,
  He will by no means believe his heart is with him
  Until he sees it: the devil is not cunning enough
  To circumvent us in riddles.
BOSOLA. Will you reject that noble and free league
  Of amity and love which I present you?
DUCHESS. Their league is like that of some politic kings,
  Only to make themselves of strength and power
  To be our after-ruin: tell them so.
BOSOLA. And what from you?
ANTONIO. Thus tell him; I will not come.
BOSOLA. And what of this?
ANTONIO. My brothers have dispersed
  Blood-hounds abroad; which till I hear are muzzled,
  No truce, though hatched with ne'er such politic skill,
  Is safe, that hangs upon our enemies' will.
  I'll not come at them.
BOSOLA. This proclaims your breeding:
  Every small thing draws a base mind to fear,
  As the adamant draws iron. Fare you well, sir:
  You shall shortly hear from 's.   [*Exit*
DUCHESS. I suspect some ambush:
  Therefore by all my love I do conjure you
  To take your eldest son, and fly towards Milan.
  Let us not venture all this poor remainder
  In one unlucky bottom.
ANTONIO. You counsel safely.
  Best of my life, farewell, since we must part:
  Heaven hath a hand in 't; but no otherwise
  Then as some curious artist takes in sunder

A clock or watch, when it is out of frame,
To bring 't in better order.
DUCHESS. I know not which is best,
To see you dead, or part with you.—Farewell, boy:
Thou art happy that thou hast not understanding
To know thy misery; for all our wit
And reading brings us to a truer sense
Of sorrow.—In the eternal church, sir,
I do hope we shall not part thus.
ANTONIO. O, be of comfort!
Make patience a noble fortitude,
And think not how unkindly we are used:
Man, like to cassia,[42] is proved best being bruised.
DUCHESS. Must I, like a slave-born Russian,
Account it praise to suffer tyranny?
And yet, O Heaven, thy heavy hand is in 't!
I have seen my little boy oft scourge his top,
And compared myself to 't: naught made me e'er
Go right but Heaven's scourge-stick.
ANTONIO. Do not weep:
Heaven fashioned us of nothing, and we strive
To bring ourselves to nothing.—Farewell, Cariola,
And thy sweet armful.—If I do never see thee more,
Be a good mother to your little ones,
And save them from the tiger: fare you well.
DUCHESS. Let me look upon you once more, for that speech
Came from a dying father: your kiss is colder
Than that I have seen a holy anchorite
Give to a dead man's skull.
ANTONIO. My heart is turned to a heavy lump of lead,
With which I sound my danger: fare you well.

Exeunt ANTONIO *and his* SON.

DUCHESS. My laurel is all withered.
CARIOLA. Look, madam, what a troop of armèd men
Make towards us.
DUCHESS. O, they are very welcome:
When Fortune's wheel is over-charged with princes,
The weight makes it move swift: I would have my ruin
Be sudden.

---

[42]A medicinal bark.

Re-enter BOSOLA *visarded,*[43] *with a* GUARD.

I am your adventure,[44] am I not?
BOSOLA. You are: you must see your husband no more.
DUCHESS. What devil art thou that counterfeit'st
  Heaven's thunder?
BOSOLA. Is that terrible? I would have you tell me whether
  Is that note worse that frights the silly birds
  Out of the corn, or that which doth allure them
  To the nets? you have hearkened to the last too much.
DUCHESS. O misery! like to a rusty o'ercharged cannon,
  Shall I never fly in pieces?—Come, to what prison?
BOSOLA. To none.
DUCHESS. Whither, then?
BOSOLA. To your palace.
DUCHESS. I have heard
  That Charon's boat serves to convey all o'er
  The dismal lake, but brings none back again.
BOSOLA. Your brothers mean you safety and pity.
DUCHESS. Pity!
  With such a pity men preserve alive
  Pheasants and quails, when they are not fat enough
  To be eaten.
BOSOLA. These are your children?
DUCHESS. Yes.
BOSOLA. Can they prattle?
DUCHESS. No;
  But I intend, since they were born accursed,
  Curses shall be their first language.
BOSOLA. Fie, madam!
  Forget this base, low fellow,—
DUCHESS. Were I a man,
  I'd beat that counterfeit face into thy other.
BOSOLA. One of no birth.
DUCHESS. Say that he was born mean,
  Man is most happy when 's own actions
  Be arguments and examples of his virtue.
BOSOLA. A barren, beggarly virtue.
DUCHESS. I prithee, who is greatest? can you tell?
  Sad tales befit my woe: I'll tell you one.

---

[43]Visored or masked.
[44]Quarry.

A salmon, as she swam unto the sea,
Met with a dog-fish, who encounters her
With this rough language: "Why art thou so bold
To mix thyself with our high state of floods,
Being no eminent courtier, but one
That for the calmest and fresh time o' the year
Dost live in shallow rivers, rank'st thyself
With silly smelts and shrimps? and darest thou
Pass by our dog-ship without reverence?"
"O!" quoth the salmon, "sister, be at peace:
Thank Jupiter we both have passed the net!
Our value never can be truly known,
Till in the fisher's basket we be shown:
I' the market then my price may be the higher,
Even when I am nearest to the cook and fire."
So to great men the moral may be stretched;
Men oft are valued high, when they're most wretched.—
But come, whither you please. I am armed 'gainst misery;
Bent to all sways of the oppressor's will:
There's no deep valley but near some great hill.   [*Exeunt*

ACT IV

Scene I

An apartment in the DUCHESS's *palace at Malfi.*

Enter FERDINAND *and* BOSOLA.

FERDINAND. How doth our sister duchess bear herself
   In her imprisonment?
BOSOLA. Nobly: I'll describe her.
   She's sad as one long used to 't, and she seems
   Rather to welcome the end of misery
   Than shun it; a behavior so noble
   As gives a majesty to adversity:
   You may discern the shape of loveliness
   More perfect in her tears than in her smiles:
   She will muse four hours together; and her silence,
   Methinks, expresseth more than if she spake.
FERDINAND. Her melancholy seems to be fortified
   With a strange disdain.
BOSOLA. 'Tis so; and this restraint,
   Like English mastiffs that grow fierce with tying,
   Makes her too passionately apprehend
   Those pleasures she's kept from.
FERDINAND. Curse upon her!
   I will no longer study in the book
   Of another's heart. Inform her what I told you.   [*Exit*

Enter DUCHESS.

BOSOLA. All comfort to your grace!
DUCHESS. I will have none.
   Pray thee, why dost thou wrap thy poisoned pills

55

In gold and sugar?

BOSOLA. Your elder brother, the Lord Ferdinand,
Is come to visit you, and sends you word,
'Cause once he rashly made a solemn vow
Never to see you more, he comes i' the night;
And prays you gently neither torch nor taper
Shine in your chamber: he will kiss your hand,
And reconcile himself; but for his vow
He dares not see you.

DUCHESS. At his pleasure.—
Take hence the lights.—He's come.

Enter FERDINAND.

FERDINAND. Where are you?

DUCHESS. Here, sir.

FERDINAND. This darkness suits you well.

DUCHESS. I would ask your pardon.

FERDINAND. You have it;
For I account it the honorabl'st revenge,
Where I may kill, to pardon.—Where are your cubs?

DUCHESS. Whom?

FERDINAND. Call them your children;
For though our national law distinguish bastards
From true legitimate issue, compassionate nature
Makes them all equal.

DUCHESS. Do you visit me for this?
You violate a sacrament o' the church
Shall make you howl in hell for 't.

FERDINAND. It had been well,
Could you have lived thus always; for, indeed,
You were too much i' the light:—but no more:
I come to seal my peace with you. Here's a hand
                          [*Gives her a dead man's hand*
To which you have vowed much love; the ring upon 't
You gave.

DUCHESS. I affectionately kiss it.

FERDINAND. Pray, do, and bury the print of it in your heart.
I will leave this ring with you for a love-token;
And the hand as sure as the ring; and do not doubt
But you shall have the heart too: when you need a friend,
Send it to him that owned it; you shall see
Whether he can aid you.

DUCHESS. You are very cold:
  I fear you are not well after your travel.—
  Ha! lights!—O, horrible!
FERDINAND. Let her have lights enough.   [*Exit*
DUCHESS. What witchcraft doth he practice, that he hath left
  A dead man's hand here?

Here is discovered, behind a traverse,[45] *the artificial figures of*
ANTONIO *and his* CHILDREN, *appearing as if they were dead.*

BOSOLA. Look you, here's the piece from which 'twas ta'en.
  He doth present you this sad spectacle,
  That, now you know directly they are dead,
  Hereafter you may wisely cease to grieve
  For that which cannot be recoverèd.
DUCHESS. There is not between Heaven and earth one wish
  I stay for after this: it wastes me more
  Than were 't my picture, fashioned out of wax,
  Stuck with a magical needle, and then buried
  In some foul dunghill; and yond's an excellent property
  For a tyrant, which I would account mercy.
BOSOLA. What's that?
DUCHESS. If they would bind me to that lifeless trunk,
  And let me freeze to death.
BOSOLA. Come, you must live.
DUCHESS. That's the greatest torture souls feel in hell,
  In hell, that they must live, and cannot die.
  Portia,[46] I'll new kindle thy coals again,
  And revive the rare and almost dead example
  Of a loving wife.
BOSOLA. O, fie! despair? remember
  You are a Christian.
DUCHESS. The church enjoins fasting:
  I'll starve myself to death.
BOSOLA. Leave this vain sorrow.
  Things being at the worst begin to mend: the bee
  When he hath shot his sting into your hand,
  May then play with your eyelid.

---

[45]A curtain.
[46]Brutus's wife, who committed suicide by casting burning coals into her mouth and
  choking herself with them after the death of Brutus at Philippi.

DUCHESS. Good comfortable fellow,
　Persuade a wretch that's broke upon the wheel
　To have all his bones new set; entreat him live
　To be executed again. Who must despatch me?
　I account this world a tedious theater,
　For I do play a part in 't 'gainst my will.
BOSOLA. Come, be of comfort; I will save your life.
DUCHESS. Indeed, I have not leisure to tend
　So small a business.
BOSOLA. Now, by my life, I pity you.
DUCHESS. Thou art a fool, then,
　To waste thy pity on a thing so wretched
　As cannot pity itself. I am full of daggers.
　Puff, let me blow these vipers from me.

Enter SERVANT.

　What are you?
SERVANT. One that wishes you long life.
DUCHESS. I would thou wert hanged for the horrible curse
　Thou hast given me: I shall shortly grow one
　Of the miracles of pity. I'll go pray;—
　No, I'll go curse.
BOSOLA. O, fie!
DUCHESS. I could curse the stars.
BOSOLA. O, fearful.
DUCHESS. And those three smiling seasons of the year
　Into a Russian winter: nay, the world
　To its first chaos.
BOSOLA. Look you, the stars shine still.
DUCHESS. O, but you must
　Remember, my curse hath a great way to go.—
　Plagues, that make lanes through largest families,
　Consume them!—
BOSOLA. Fie, lady!
DUCHESS. Let them, like tyrants,
　Never be remembered but for the ill they have done;
　Let all the zealous prayers of mortified
　Churchmen forget them!—
BOSOLA. O, uncharitable!
DUCHESS. Let Heaven a little while cease crowning martyrs,
　To punish them!—

[handwritten annotation: She curses!]

[handwritten annotation: —She has reached dispair — the inability to accept grace]

Go, howl them this, and say, I long to bleed:
It is some mercy when men kill with speed.   [*Exit*

Re-enter FERDINAND.

FERDINAND. Excellent, as I would wish; she's plagued in art:
  These presentations are but framed in wax
  By the curious master in that quality,
  Vincentio Lauriola, and she takes them
  For true substantial bodies.
BOSOLA. Why do you do this?
FERDINAND. To bring her to despair.
BOSOLA. Faith, end here,
  And go no farther in your cruelty:
  Send her a penitential garment to put on
  Next to her delicate skin, and furnish her
  With beads and prayer-books.
FERDINAND. Damn her! that body of hers,
  While that my blood ran pure in 't, was more worth
  Than that which thou wouldst comfort, called a soul.
  I will send her masks of common courtezans,
  Have her meat served up by bawds and ruffians,
  And, 'cause she'll needs be mad, I am resolved
  To remove forth the common hospital
  All the mad-folk, and place them near her lodging;
  There let them practice together, sing and dance,
  And act their gambols to the full o' the moon:
  If she can sleep the better for it, let her.
  Your work is almost ended.
BOSOLA. Must I see her again?
FERDINAND. Yes.
BOSOLA. Never.
FERDINAND. You must.
BOSOLA. Never in mine own shape;
  That's forfeited by my intelligence
  And this last cruel lie: when you send me next,
  The business shall be comfort.
FERDINAND. Very likely;
  Thy pity is nothing of kin to thee. Antonio
  Lurks about Milan: thou shalt shortly thither,
  To feed a fire as great as my revenge,
  Which never will slack till it have spent his fuel:
  Intemperate agues make physicians cruel.   [*Exeunt*

Scene II

Another room in the DUCHESS's *lodging.*

Enter DUCHESS *and* CARIOLA.

DUCHESS. What hideous noise was that?
CARIOLA. 'Tis the wild consort
  Of madmen, lady, which your tyrant brother
  Hath placed about your lodging: this tyranny,
  I think, was never practiced till this hour.
DUCHESS. Indeed, I thank him: nothing but noise and folly
  Can keep me in my right wits; whereas reason
  And silence make me stark mad. Sit down;
  Discourse to me some dismal tragedy.
CARIOLA. O, 'twill increase your melancholy.
DUCHESS. Thou art deceived:
  To hear of greater grief would lessen mine.
  This is a prison?
CARIOLA. Yes, but you shall live
  To shake this durance off.
DUCHESS. Thou art a fool:
  The robin-redbreast and the nightingale
  Never live long in cages.
CARIOLA. Pray, dry your eyes.
  What think you of, madam?
DUCHESS. Of nothing;
  When I muse thus, I sleep.
CARIOLA. Like a madman, with your eyes open?
DUCHESS. Dost thou think we shall know one another
  In the other world?
CARIOLA. Yes, out of question.
DUCHESS. O, that it were possible we might
  But hold some two days' conference with the dead!
  From them I should learn somewhat, I am sure,
  I never shall know here. I'll tell thee a miracle;
  I am not mad yet, to my cause of sorrow:
  The Heaven o'er my head seems made of molten brass,
  The earth of flaming sulphur, yet I am not mad.
  I am acquainted with sad misery
  As the tanned galley-slave is with his oar;
  Necessity makes me suffer constantly,
  And custom makes it easy. Who do I look like now?

CARIOLA. Like to your picture in the gallery,
    A deal of life in show, but none in practice;
    Or rather like some reverend monument
    Whose ruins are even pitied.
DUCHESS. Very proper;
    And Fortune seems only to have her eyesight
    To behold my tragedy.—How now!
    What noise is that?

Enter SERVANT.

SERVANT. I am come to tell you
    Your brother hath intended you some sport.
    A great physician, when the Pope was sick
    Of a deep melancholy, presented him
    With several sorts of madmen, which wild object
    Being full of change and sport, forced him to laugh,
    And so the imposthume[47] broke: the self-same cure
    The duke intends on you.
DUCHESS. Let them come in.
SERVANT. There's a mad lawyer; and a secular priest;
    A doctor that hath forfeited his wits
    By jealousy; an astrologian
    That in his works said such a day o' the month
    Should be the day of doom, and, failing of 't,
    Ran mad; an English tailor crazed i' the brain
    With the study of new fashions; a gentleman-usher
    Quite beside himself with care to keep in mind
    The number of his lady's salutations
    Or "How do you" she employed him in each morning;
    A farmer, too, an excellent knave in grain,
    Mad 'cause he was hindered transportation:
    And let one broker that's mad loose to these,
    You'd think the devil were among them.
DUCHESS. Sit, Cariola.—Let them loose when you please,
    For I am chained to endure all your tyranny.

Enter MADMEN. *Here this song is sung to a dismal kind of music by a* MADMAN.

---

[47]Ulcer.

O, let us howl some heavy note,
  Some deadly doggèd howl,
Sounding as from the threatening throat
  Of beasts and fatal fowl!
As ravens, screech-owls, bulls, and bears,
  We'll bell, and bawl our parts,
Till irksome noise have cloyed your ears
  And còrrosived your hearts.
At last, when as our choir wants breath,
  Our bodies being blest,
We'll sing, like swans, to welcome death,
  And die in love and rest.

1ST MADMAN. Doom's-day not come yet! I'll draw it nearer by a perspective, or make a glass that shall set all the world on fire upon an instant. I cannot sleep; my pillow is stuffed with a litter of porcupines.

2ND MADMAN. Hell is a mere glass-house, where the devils are continually blowing up women's souls on hollow irons, and the fire never goes out.

3RD MADMAN. I will lie with every woman in my parish the tenth night; I will tythe them over like haycocks.

4TH MADMAN. Shall my pothecary out-go me because I am a cuckold? I have found out his roguery; he makes alum of his wife's urine, and sells it to Puritans that have sore throats with overstraining.

1ST MADMAN. I have skill in heraldry.

2ND MADMAN. Hast?

1ST MADMAN. You do give for your crest a woodcock's head with the brains picked out on 't; you are a very ancient gentleman.

3RD MADMAN. Greek is turned Turk: we are only to be saved by the Helvetian translation.[48]

1ST MADMAN. Come on, sir, I will lay the law to you.

2ND MADMAN. O, rather lay a corrosive: the law will eat to the bone.

3RD MADMAN. He that drinks but to satisfy nature is damned.

4TH MADMAN. If I had my glass here, I would show a sight should make all the women here call me mad doctor.

1ST MADMAN. What's he? a rope-maker?

2ND MADMAN. No, no, no, a snuffling knave that, while he shows the tombs, will have his hand in a wench's placket.

3RD MADMAN. Woe to the caroche that brought home my wife from the masque at three o'clock in the morning! it had a large feather-bed in it.

---

[48]The Genevan Bible, a translation made by Puritan exiles in 1560.

4TH MADMAN. I have pared the devil's nails forty times, roasted them in raven's eggs, and cured agues with them.

3RD MADMAN. Get me three hundred milch-bats, to make possets to procure sleep.

4TH MADMAN. All the college may throw their caps at me: I have made a soap-boiler costive;[49] it was my masterpiece.

Here a dance of EIGHT MADMEN, *with music answerable thereto; after which,* BOSOLA, *like an* OLD MAN, *enters.*

DUCHESS. Is he mad too?

SERVANT. Pray, question him. I'll leave you.

Exeunt SERVANT *and* MADMEN.

BOSOLA. I am come to make thy tomb.

DUCHESS. Ha! my tomb!
Thou speak'st as if I lay upon my deathbed,
Gasping for breath: dost thou perceive me sick?

BOSOLA. Yes, and the more dangerously, since thy sickness is insensible.

DUCHESS. Thou art not mad, sure: dost know me?

BOSOLA. Yes.

DUCHESS. Who am I?

BOSOLA. Thou art a box of worm-seed, at best but a salvatory of green mummy. What's this flesh? a little crudded[50] milk, fantastical puff-paste. Our bodies are weaker than those paper-prisons boys use to keep flies in; more contemptible, since ours is to preserve earth-worms. Didst thou ever see a lark in a cage? Such is the soul in the body: this world is like her little turf of grass, and the Heaven o'er our heads, like her looking-glass, only gives us a miserable knowledge of the small compass of our prison.

DUCHESS. Am not I thy duchess?

BOSOLA. Thou art some great woman, sure, for riot begins to sit on thy forehead (clad in gray hairs) twenty years sooner than on a merry milkmaid's. Thou sleepest worse than if a mouse should be forced to take up her lodging in a cat's ear: a little infant that breeds its teeth, should it lie with thee, would cry out, as if thou wert the more un-quiet bedfellow.

DUCHESS. I am Duchess of Malfi still.

BOSOLA. That makes thy sleeps so broken:
Glories, like glow-worms, afar off shine bright,
But looked to near, have neither heat nor light.

---

[49]Constipated.
[50]Curdled.

DUCHESS. Thou art very plain.

BOSOLA. My trade is to flatter the dead, not the living;
I am a tomb-maker.

DUCHESS. And thou comest to make my tomb?

BOSOLA. Yes.

DUCHESS. Let me be a little merry:—of what stuff wilt thou make it?

BOSOLA. Nay, resolve me first, of what fashion?

DUCHESS. Why do we grow fantastical in our deathbeds? do we affect fashion in the grave?

BOSOLA. Most ambitiously. Princes' images on their tombs do not lie, as they were wont, seeming to pray up to Heaven; but with their hands under their cheeks, as if they died of the toothache: they are not carved with their eyes fixed upon the stars; but as their minds were wholly bent upon the world, the self-same way they seem to turn their faces.

DUCHESS. Let me know fully therefore the effect
Of this thy dismal preparation,
This talk fit for a charnel.

BOSOLA. Now I shall:—

Enter EXECUTIONERS, *with a coffin, cords, and a bell.*

Here is a present from your princely brothers;
And may it arrive welcome, for it brings
Last benefit, last sorrow.

DUCHESS. Let me see it:
I have so much obedience in my blood,
I wish it in their veins to do them good.

BOSOLA. This is your last presence-chamber.

CARIOLA. O my sweet lady!

DUCHESS. Peace; it affrights not me.

BOSOLA. I am the common bellman,
That usually is sent to condemned persons
The night before they suffer.

DUCHESS. Even now thou said 'st
Thou wast a tomb-maker.

BOSOLA. 'Twas to bring you
By degrees to mortification. Listen.

Hark, now every thing is still
The screech-owl and the whistler shrill
Call upon our dame aloud,
And bid her quickly don her shroud!
Much you had of land and rent;
Your length in clay's now competent:

A long war disturbed your mind;
Here your perfect peace is signed.
Of what is 't fools make such vain keeping?
Sin their conception, their birth weeping,
Their life a general mist of error,
Their death a hideous storm of terror.
Strew your hair with powders sweet,
Don clean linen, bathe your feet,
And (the foul fiend more to check)
A crucifix let bless your neck:
'Tis now full tide 'tween night and day;
End your groan, and come away.

CARIOLA. Hence, villains, tyrants, murderers! alas!
  What will you do with my lady?—Call for help.
DUCHESS. To whom? to our next neighbors? they are mad-folks.
BOSOLA. Remove that noise.
DUCHESS. Farewell, Cariola.
  In my last will I have not much to give:
  A many hungry guests have fed upon me;
  Thine will be a poor reversion.[51]
CARIOLA. I will die with her.
DUCHESS. I pray thee, look thou giv'st my little boy
  Some syrup for his cold, and let the girl
  Say her prayers ere she sleep.

CARIOLA *is forced out by the* EXECUTIONERS.

  Now what you please:
  What death?
BOSOLA. Strangling; here are your executioners.
DUCHESS. I forgive them:
  The apoplexy, catarrh, or cough o' the lungs
  Would do as much as they do.
BOSOLA. Doth not death fright you?
DUCHESS. Who would be afraid on 't,
  Knowing to meet such excellent company
  In the other world?
BOSOLA. Yet, methinks,
  The manner of your death should much afflict you:
  This cord should terrify you.
DUCHESS. Not a whit:
  What would it pleasure me to have my throat cut
  With diamonds? or to be smotherèd

---

[51]Residue.

With cassia? or to be shot to death with pearls?
I know death hath ten thousand several doors
For men to take their exits; and 'tis found
They go on such strange geometrical hinges,
You may open them both ways; any way, for Heaven sake,
So I were out of your whispering. Tell my brothers
That I perceive death, now I am well awake,
Best gift is they can give or I can take.
I would fain put off my last woman's fault,
I'd not be tedious to you.
1ST EXECUTIONER. We are ready.
DUCHESS. Dispose my breath how please you; but body
Bestow upon my women, will you?
1ST EXECUTIONER. Yes.
DUCHESS. Pull, and pull strongly, for your able strength
Must pull down Heaven upon me:—
Yet stay; Heaven-gates are not so highly arched
As princes' palaces; they that enter there
Must go upon their knees. [Kneels]—Come, violent death,
Serve for mandragora to make me sleep!—
Go tell my brothers, when I am laid out,
They then may feed in quiet.

The EXECUTIONERS strangle the DUCHESS.

BOSOLA. Where's the waiting woman?
Fetch her: some other strangle the children.

CARIOLA and CHILDREN are brought in by the EXECUTIONERS; who
presently strangle the CHILDREN.

Look you, there sleeps your mistress.
CARIOLA. O, you are damned
Perpetually for this! My turn is next,
Is 't not so ordered?
BOSOLA. Yes, and I am glad
You are so well prepared for 't.
CARIOLA. You are deceived, sir,
I am not prepared for 't, I will not die;
I will first come to my answer, and know
How I have offended.
BOSOLA. Come, despatch her.—
You kept her counsel; now you shall keep ours.
CARIOLA. I will not die, I must not; I am contracted
To a young gentleman.

1ST EXECUTIONER. Here's your wedding-ring.
CARIOLA. Let me but speak with the duke; I'll discover
    Treason to his person.
BOSOLA. Delays: — throttle her.
1ST EXECUTIONER. She bites and scratches.
CARIOLA. If you kill me now,
    I am damned; I have not been at confession
    This two years.
BOSOLA. [*To* EXECUTIONERS] When?
CARIOLA. I am quick with child.
BOSOLA. Why, then,
    Your credit's saved.

The EXECUTIONERS *strangle* CARIOLA.

Bear her into the next room;
Let these lie still.

Exeunt the EXECUTIONERS *with the body of* CARIOLA. *Enter*
FERDINAND.

FERDINAND. Is she dead?
BOSOLA. She is what
    You'd have her. But here begin your pity.
                                    [*Shows the* CHILDREN *strangled*
    Alas, how have these offended?
FERDINAND. The death
    Of young wolves is never to be pitied.
BOSOLA. Fix your eye here.
FERDINAND. Constantly.
BOSOLA. Do you not weep?
    Other sins only speak; murder shrieks out:
    The element of water moistens the earth,
    But blood flies upwards and bedews the heavens.
FERDINAND. Cover her face; mine eyes dazzle: she died young.
BOSOLA. I think not so; her infelicity
    Seemed to have years too many.
FERDINAND. She and I were twins;
    And should I die this instant, I have lived
    Her time to a minute.
BOSOLA. It seems she was born first:
    You have bloodily approved the ancient truth,
    That kindred commonly do worse agree
    Than remote strangers.
FERDINAND. Let me see her face

Again. Why didst not thou pity her? what
An excellent honest man mightst thou have been,
If thou hadst borne her to some sanctuary!
Or, bold in a good cause, opposed thyself,
With thy advancèd sword above thy head,
Between her innocence and my revenge!
I bade thee, when I was distracted of my wits,
Go kill my dearest friend, and thou hast done 't.
For let me but examine well the cause:
What was the meanness of her match to me?
Only I must confess I had a hope,
Had she continued widow, to have gained
An infinite mass of treasure by her death:
And what was the main cause? her marriage,
That drew a stream of gall quite through my heart.
For thee, as we observe in tragedies
That a good actor many times is cursed
For playing a villain's part, I hate thee for 't,
And, for my sake, say, thou hast done much ill well.
BOSOLA. Let me quicken your memory, for I perceive
   You are falling into ingratitude: I challenge
   The reward due to my service.
FERDINAND. I'll tell thee
   What I'll give thee.
BOSOLA. Do.
FERDINAND. I'll give thee a pardon
   For this murder.
BOSOLA. Ha!
FERDINAND. Yes, and 'tis
   The largest bounty I can study to do thee.
   By what authority didst thou execute
   This bloody sentence?
BOSOLA. By yours.
FERDINAND. Mine! was I her judge?
   Did any ceremonial form of law
   Doom her to not-being? did a còmplete jury
   Deliver her conviction up i' the court?
   Where shalt thou find this judgment registered,
   Unless in hell? See, like a bloody fool,
   Thou'st forfeited thy life, and thou shalt die for 't.
BOSOLA. The office of justice is perverted quite
   When one thief hangs another. Who shall dare
   To reveal this?

FERDINAND. O, I'll tell thee;
  The wolf shall find her grave, and scrape it up,
  Not to devour the corpse, but to discover
  The horrid murder.
BOSOLA. You, not I, shall quake for 't.
FERDINAND. Leave me.
BOSOLA. I will first receive my pension.
FERDINAND. You are a villain.
BOSOLA. When your ingratitude
  Is judge, I am so.
FERDINAND. O horror,
  That not the fear of him which binds the devils
  Can prescribe man obedience!—
  Never look upon me more.
BOSOLA. Why, fare thee well.
  Your brother and yourself are worthy men:
  You have a pair of hearts are hollow graves,
  Rotten, and rotting others; and your vengeance,
  Like two chained bullets, still goes arm in arm:
  You may be brothers; for treason, like the plague,
  Doth take much in a blood. I stand like one
  That long hath ta'en a sweet and golden dream:
  I am angry with myself, now that I wake.
FERDINAND. Get thee into some unknown part o' the world,
  That I may never see thee.
BOSOLA. Let me know
  Wherefore I should be thus neglected. Sir,
  I served your tyranny, and rather strove
  To satisfy yourself than all the world:
  And though I loathed the evil, yet I loved
  You that did counsel it; and rather sought
  To appear a true servant than an honest man.
FERDINAND. I'll go hunt the badger by owl-light.
  'Tis a deed of darkness.   [Exit
BOSOLA. He's much distracted. Off, my painted honor!
  While with vain hopes our faculties we tire,
  We seem to sweat in ice and freeze in fire.
  What would I do, were this to do again?
  I would not change my peace of conscience
  For all the wealth of Europe.—She stirs; here's life:—
  Return, fair soul, from darkness, and lead mine
  Out of this sensible hell:—she's warm, she breathes:—
  Upon thy pale lips I will melt my heart,

To store them with fresh color.—Who's there!
Some cordial drink!—Alas! I dare not call:
So pity would destroy pity.—Her eye opes,
And Heaven in it seems to ope, that late was shut,
To take me up to mercy.
DUCHESS. Antonio!
BOSOLA. Yes, madam, he is living;
   The dead bodies you saw were but feigned statues:
   He's reconciled to your brothers; the Pope hath wrought
   The atonement.
DUCHESS. Mercy!   [*Dies*
BOSOLA. O, she's gone again! there the cords of life broke.
   O sacred innocence, that sweetly sleeps
   On turtles' feathers, whilst a guilty conscience
   Is a black register wherein is writ
   All our good deeds and bad, a perspective
   That shows us hell! That we cannot be suffered
   To do good when we have a mind to it!
   This is manly sorrow;
   These tears, I am very certain, never grew
   In my mother's milk: my estate has sunk
   Below the degree of fear: where were
   These penitent fountains while she was living?
   O, they were frozen up! Here is a sight
   As direful to my soul as is the sword
   Unto a wretch has slain his father. Come,
   I'll bear thee hence,
   And execute thy last will; that's deliver
   Thy body to the reverend dispose
   Of some good women: that the cruel tyrant
   Shall not deny me. Then I'll post to Milan,
   Where somewhat I will speedily enact
   Worth my dejection.   [*Exit*

ACT V

Scene I

A public place in Milan.

Enter ANTONIO *and* DELIO.

ANTONIO. What think you of my hope of reconcilement
    To the Aragonian brethren?
DELIO. I misdoubt it;
    For though they have sent their letters of safe-conduct
    For your repair to Milan, they appear
    But nets to entrap you. The Marquis of Pescara,
    Under whom you hold certain land in cheat,[52]
    Much 'gainst his noble nature hath been moved
    To seize those lands; and some of his dependents
    Are at this instant making it their suit
    To be invested in your revenues.
    I cannot think they mean well to your life
    That do deprive you of your means of life,
    Your living.
ANTONIO. You are still an heretic
    To any safety I can shape myself.
DELIO. Here comes the marquis: I will make myself
    Petitioner for some part of your land,
    To know whither it is flying.
ANTONIO. I pray do.

    Enter PESCARA.

DELIO. Sir, I have a suit to you.

---

[52]Subject to escheat.

71

PESCARA. To me?
DELIO. An easy one:
　There is the citadel of Saint Bennet,
　With some demesnes, of late in the possession
　Of Antonio Bologna,—please you bestow them on me.
PESCARA. You are my friend; but this is such a suit,
　Nor fit for me to give, nor you to take.
DELIO. No, sir?
PESCARA. I will give you ample reason for 't
　Soon in private:—here's the cardinal's mistress.

Enter JULIA.

JULIA. My lord, I am grown your poor petitioner,
　And should be an ill beggar, had I not
　A great man's letter here, the cardinal's,
　To court you in my favor.　　　　　　　　　　　　[*Gives a letter*
PESCARA. He entreats for you
　The citadel of Saint Bennet, that belonged
　To the banished Bologna.
JULIA. Yes.
PESCARA. I could not have thought of a friend I could rather
　Pleasure with it: 'tis yours.
JULIA. Sir, I thank you;
　And he shall know how doubly I am engaged
　Both in your gift, and speediness of giving
　Which makes your grant the greater.　　　　　　　　[*Exit*
ANTONIO. How they fortify
　Themselves with my ruin!
DELIO. Sir, I am
　Little bound to you.
PESCARA. Why?
DELIO. Because you denied this suit to me, and gave 't
　To such a creature.
PESCARA. Do you know what it was?
　It was Antonio's land; not forfeited
　By course of law, but ravished from his throat
　By the cardinal's entreaty: it were not fit
　I should bestow so main a piece of wrong
　Upon my friend; 'tis a gratification
　Only due to a strumpet, for it is injustice.
　Shall I sprinkle the pure blood of innocents
　To make those followers I call my friends
　Look ruddier upon me? I am glad

This land, ta'en from the owner by such wrong,
Returns again unto so foul an use
As salary for his lust. Learn, good Delio,
To ask noble things of me, and you shall find
I'll be a noble giver.
DELIO. You instruct me well.
ANTONIO. Why, here's a man who would fright impudence
    From sauciest beggars.
PESCARA. Prince Ferdinand's come to Milan,
    Sick, as they give out, of an apoplexy;
    But some say 'tis a frenzy: I am going
    To visit him.   [Exit
ANTONIO. 'Tis a noble old fellow.
DELIO. What course do you mean to take, Antonio?
ANTONIO. This night I mean to venture all my fortune,
    Which is no more than a poor lingering life,
    To the cardinal's worst of malice: I have got
    Private access to his chamber; and intend
    To visit him about the mid of night,
    As once his brother did our noble duchess.
    It may be that the sudden apprehension
    Of danger,—for I'll go in mine own shape,—
    When he shall see it fraight with love and duty,
    May draw the poison out of him, and work
    A friendly reconcilement: if it fail,
    Yet it shall rid me of this infamous calling;
    For better fall once than be ever falling.
DELIO. I'll second you in all danger; and, howe'er,
    My life keeps rank with yours.
ANTONIO. You are still my loved and best friend.   [Exeunt

Scene II

A gallery in the CARDINAL's *palace at Milan.*

Enter PESCARA *and* DOCTOR.

PESCARA. Now, doctor, may I visit your patient?
DOCTOR. If 't please your lordship: but he's instantly
    To take the air here in the gallery
    By my direction.
PESCARA. Pray thee, what's his disease?
DOCTOR. A very pestilent disease, my lord,

They call lycanthropia.
PESCARA. What's that?
I need a dictionary to 't.
DOCTOR. I'll tell you.
In those that are possessed with 't there o'erflows
Such melancholy humor they imagine
Themselves to be transformed into wolves;
Steal forth to churchyards in the dead of night,
And dig dead bodies up: as two nights since
One met the duke 'bout midnight in a lane
Behind Saint Mark's church, with the leg of a man
Upon his shoulder; and he howled fearfully;
Said he was a wolf, only the difference
Was, a wolf's skin was hairy on the outside,
His on the inside; bade them take their swords,
Rip up his flesh, and try: straight I was sent for,
And, having ministered to him, found his grace
Very well recovered.
PESCARA. I am glad on 't.
DOCTOR. Yet not without some fear
Of a relapse. If he grow to his fit again,
I'll go a nearer way to work with him
Than ever Paracelsus[53] dreamed of; if
They'll give me leave, I'll buffet his madness out of him.
Stand aside; he comes.

Enter FERDINAND, CARDINAL, MALATESTI, *and* BOSOLA.

FERDINAND. Leave me.
MALATESTI. Why doth your lordship love this solitariness?
FERDINAND. Eagles commonly fly alone; they are crows, daws, and star-
lings that flock together. Look, what's that follows me?
MALATESTI. Nothing, my lord.
FERDINAND. Yes.
MALATESTI. 'Tis your shadow.
FERDINAND. Stay it; let it not haunt me.
MALATESTI. Impossible, if you move, and the sun shine.
FERDINAND. I will throttle it.   [*Throws himself down on his shadow*
MALATESTI. O, my lord, you are angry with nothing.
FERDINAND. You are a fool: how is 't possible I should catch my shadow,
unless I fall upon 't? When I go to hell, I mean to carry a bribe; for,
look you, good gifts evermore make way for the worst persons.

[53]Physician and alchemist (1493?–1541).

PESCARA. Rise, good my lord.

FERDINAND. I am studying the art of patience.

PESCARA. 'Tis a noble virtue.

FERDINAND. To drive six snails before me from this town to Moscow; neither use goad nor whip to them, but let them take their own time;—the patient'st man i' the world match me for an experiment;—and I'll crawl after like a sheep-biter.

CARDINAL. Force him up.

They raise him.

FERDINAND. Use me well, you were best. What I have done, I have done: I'll confess nothing.

DOCTOR. Now let me come to him.—Are you mad, my lord? are you out of your princely wits?

FERDINAND. What's he?

PESCARA. Your doctor.

FERDINAND. Let me have his beard sawed off, and his eyebrows filed more civil.

DOCTOR. I must do mad tricks with him, for that's the only way on 't.— I have brought your grace a salamander's skin to keep you from sun-burning.

FERDINAND. I have cruel sore eyes.

DOCTOR. The white of a cockatrix's egg is present remedy.

FERDINAND. Let it be a new laid one, you were best.— Hide me from him: physicians are like kings,— They brook no contradiction.

DOCTOR. Now he begins to fear me: now let me alone with him.

CARDINAL. How now! put off your gown!

DOCTOR. Let me have some forty urinals filled with rose-water: he and I'll go pelt one another with them.—Now he begins to fear me.— Can you fetch a frisk, sir?—Let him go, let him go, upon my peril: I find by his eye he stands in awe of me; I'll make him as tame as a dormouse.

FERDINAND. Can you fetch your frisks, sir!—I will stamp him into a cullis, flay off his skin, to cover one of the anatomies[54] this rogue hath set i' the cold yonder in Barber-Surgeon's[55] hall.—Hence, hence! you are all of you like beasts for sacrifice: there's nothing left of you but tongue and belly, flattery and lechery.   [*Exit*

PESCARA. Doctor, he did not fear you thoroughly.

---

[54]Skeletons.

[55]The surgeons or barber-surgeons were given the bodies of four executed criminals each year.

DOCTOR. True; I was somewhat too forward.

BOSOLA. Mercy upon me, what a fatal judgment
  Hath fall'n upon this Ferdinand!

PESCARA. Knows your grace
  What accident hath brought unto the prince
  This strange distraction?

CARDINAL. [*Aside*] I must feign somewhat.—Thus they say it grew.
  You have heard it rumored, for these many years
  None of our family dies but there is seen
  The shape of an old woman, which is given
  By tradition to us to have been murdered
  By her nephews for her riches. Such a figure
  One night, as the prince sat up late at 's book,
  Appeared to him; when crying out for help,
  The gentlemen of 's chamber found his grace
  All on a cold sweat, altered much in face
  And language: since which apparition,
  He hath grown worse and worse, and I much fear
  He cannot live.

BOSOLA. Sir, I would speak with you.

PESCARA. We'll leave your grace,
  Wishing to the sick prince, our noble lord,
  All health of mind and body.

CARDINAL. You are most welcome.

  Exeunt PESCARA, MALATESTI, *and* DOCTOR.

  Are you come? so.—[*Aside*] This fellow must not know
  By any means I had intelligence
  In our duchess's death; for, though I counselled it,
  The full of all the engagement seemed to grow
  From Ferdinand.—Now, sir, how fares our sister?
  I do not think but sorrow makes her look
  Like to an oft-dyed garment: she shall now
  Taste comfort from me. Why do you look so wildly?
  O, the fortune of your master here the prince
  Dejects you; but be you of happy comfort:
  If you'll do one thing for me I'll entreat,
  Though he had a cold tombstone o'er his bones,
  I'd make you what you would be.

BOSOLA. Any thing;
  Give it me in a breath, and let me fly to 't:
  They that think long small expedition win,
  For musing much o' the end cannot begin.

Enter JULIA.

JULIA. Sir, will you come in to supper?
CARDINAL. I am busy; leave me.
JULIA. [*Aside*] What an excellent shape hath that fellow! ·   [*Exit*
CARDINAL. 'Tis thus. Antonio lurks here in Milan:
   Inquire him out, and kill him. While he lives,
   Our sister cannot marry; and I have thought
   Of an excellent match for her. Do this, and style me
   Thy advancement.
BOSOLA. But by what means shall I find him out?
CARDINAL. There is a gentleman called Delio
   Here in the camp, that hath been long approved
   His loyal friend. Set eye upon that fellow;
   Follow him to mass; may be Antonio,
   Although he do account religion
   But a school-name, for fashion of the world
   May accompany him; or else go inquire out
   Delio's confessor, and see if you can bribe
   Him to reveal it. There are a thousand ways
   A man might find to trace him; as to know
   What fellows haunt the Jews for taking up
   Great sums of money, for sure he's in want;
   Or else to go to the picture-makers, and learn
   Who bought her picture lately: some of these
   Happily may take.
BOSOLA. Well, I'll not freeze i' the business:
   I would see that wretched thing, Antonio,
   Above all sights i' the world.
CARDINAL. Do, and be happy.   [*Exit*
BOSOLA. This fellow doth breed basilisks in 's eyes,
   He's nothing else but murder; yet he seems
   Not to have notice of the duchess's death.
   'Tis his cunning: I must follow his example;
   There cannot be a surer way to trace
   Than that of an old fox.

Re-enter JULIA.

JULIA. So, sir, you are well met.
BOSOLA. How now!
JULIA. Nay, the doors are fast enough:
   Now, sir, I will make you confess your treachery.
BOSOLA. Treachery!

JULIA. Yes, confess to me
  Which of my women 'twas you hired to put
  Love-powder into my drink?
BOSOLA. Love-powder!
JULIA. Yes, when I was at Malfi.
  Why should I fall in love with such a face else?
  I have already suffered for thee so much pain,
  The only remedy to do me good
  Is to kill my longing.
BOSOLA. Sure, your pistol holds
  Nothing but perfumes or kissing-comfits.[56]
  Excellent lady!
  You have a pretty way on 't to discover
  Your longing. Come, come, I'll disarm you,
  And arm you thus: yet this is wondrous strange.
JULIA. Compare thy form and my eyes together,
  You'll find my love no such great miracle.
  Now you'll say
  I am wanton: this nice modesty in ladies
  Is but a troublesome familiar
  That haunts them.
BOSOLA. Know you me, I am a blunt soldier.
JULIA. The better:
  Sure, there wants fire where there are no lively sparks
  Of roughness.
BOSOLA. And I want compliment.
JULIA. Why, ignorance
  In courtship cannot make you do amiss,
  If you have a heart to do well.
BOSOLA. You are very fair.
JULIA. Nay, if you lay beauty to my charge,
  I must plead unguilty.
BOSOLA. Your bright eyes
  Carry a quiver of darts in them sharper
  Than sunbeams.
JULIA. You will mar me with commendation,
  Put yourself to the charge of courting me,
  Whereas now I woo you.
BOSOLA. [*Aside*] I have it, I will work upon this creature. —
  Let us grow most amorously familiar:

---

[56]Perfumed sugar-plums, for sweetening the breath.

If the great cardinal now should see me thus,
Would he not count me a villain?
JULIA. No; he might count me a wanton,
  Not lay a scruple of offence on you;
  For if I see and steal a diamond,
  The fault is not i' the stone, but in me the thief
  That purloins it. I am sudden with you:
  We that are great women of pleasure use to cut off
  These uncertain wishes and unquiet longings,
  And in an instant join the sweet delight
  And the pretty excuse together. Had you been i' the street,
  Under my chamber-window, even there
  I should have courted you.
BOSOLA. O, you are an excellent lady!
JULIA. Bid me do somewhat for you presently
  To express I love you.
BOSOLA. I will; and if you love me,
  Fail not to effect it.
  The cardinal is grown wondrous melancholy;
  Demand the cause, let him not put you off
  With feigned excuse; discover the main ground on 't.
JULIA. Why would you know this?
BOSOLA. I have depended on him,
  And I hear that he is fall'n in some disgrace
  With the emperor: if he be, like the mice
  That forsake falling houses, I would shift
  To other dependance.
JULIA. You shall not need
  Follow the wars: I'll be your maintenance.
BOSOLA. And I your loyal servant: but I cannot
  Leave my calling.
JULIA. Not leave an ungrateful
  General for the love of a sweet lady!
  You are like some cannot sleep in feather-beds,
  But must have blocks for their pillows.
BOSOLA. Will you do this?
JULIA. Cunningly.
BOSOLA. To-morrow I'll expect the intelligence.
JULIA. To-morrow! get you into my cabinet;
  You shall have it with you. Do not delay me,
  No more than I do you: I am like one
  That is condemned; I have my pardon promised,
  But I would see it sealed. Go, get you in:

You shall see me wind my tongue about his heart
Like a skein of silk.

Exit BOSOLA. *Re-enter* CARDINAL.

CARDINAL. Where are you?

Enter SERVANTS.

SERVANTS. Here.
CARDINAL. Let none, upon your lives, have conference
With the Prince Ferdinand, unless I know it.—
[*Aside*] In this distraction he may reveal
The murder.

Exeunt SERVANTS.

Yond's my lingering consumption:
I am weary of her, and by any means
Would be quit of.
JULIA. How now, my lord! what ails you?
CARDINAL. Nothing.
JULIA. O, you are much altered:
Come, I must be your secretary, and remove
This lead from off your bosom: what's the matter?
CARDINAL. I may not tell you.
JULIA. Are you so far in love with sorrow
You cannot part with part of it? or think you
I cannot love your grace when you are sad
As well as merry? or do you suspect
I, that have been a secret to your heart
These many winters, cannot be the same
Unto your tongue?
CARDINAL. Satisfy thy longing,—
The only way to make thee keep my counsel
Is, not to tell thee.
JULIA. Tell your echo this,
Or flatterers, that like echoes still report
What they hear though most imperfect, and not me;
For if that you be true unto yourself,
I'll know.
CARDINAL. Will you rack me?
JULIA. No, judgment shall
Draw it from you: it is an equal fault,
To tell one's secrets unto all or none.
CARDINAL. The first argues folly.

JULIA. But the last tyranny.
CARDINAL. Very well: why, imagine I have committed
  Some secret deed which I desire the world
  May never hear of.
JULIA. Therefore may not I know it?
  You have concealed for me as great a sin
  As adultery. Sir, never was occasion
  For perfect trial of my constancy
  Till now: sir, I beseech you—
CARDINAL. You'll repent it.
JULIA. Never.
CARDINAL. It hurries thee to ruin: I'll not tell thee.
  Be well advised, and think what danger 'tis
  To receive a prince's secrets: they that do,
  Had need have their breasts hooped with adamant
  To contain them. I pray thee, yet be satisfied;
  Examine thine own frailty; 'tis more easy
  To tie knots than unloose them: 'tis a secret
  That, like a lingering poison, may chance lie
  Spread in thy veins, and kill thee seven year hence.
JULIA. Now you dally with me.
CARDINAL. No more; thou shalt know it.
  By my appointment the great Duchess of Malfi
  And two of her young children, four nights since,
  Were strangled.
JULIA. O Heaven! sir, what have you done!
CARDINAL. How now? how settles this? think you your bosom
  Will be a grave dark and obscure enough
  For such a secret?
JULIA. You have undone yourself, sir.
CARDINAL. Why?
JULIA. It lies not in me to conceal it.
CARDINAL. No?
  Come, I will swear you to 't upon this book.
JULIA. Most religiously.
CARDINAL. Kiss it.

She kisses the book.

Now you shall never utter it; thy curiosity
Hath undone thee: thou 'rt poisoned with that book;
Because I knew thou couldst not keep my counsel,
I have bound thee to 't by death.

Re-enter BOSOLA.

BOSOLA. For pity-sake, hold!
CARDINAL. Ha, Bosola!
JULIA. I forgive you
   This equal piece of justice you have done;
   For I betrayed your counsel to that fellow:
   He overheard it; that was the cause I said
   It lay not in me to conceal it.
BOSOLA. O foolish woman,
   Couldst not thou have poisoned him?
JULIA. 'Tis weakness,
   Too much to think what should have been done.
   I go,
   I know not whither.   [*Dies*
CARDINAL. Wherefore com'st thou hither?
BOSOLA. That I might find a great man like yourself,
   Not out of his wits as the Lord Ferdinand,
   To remember my service.
CARDINAL. I'll have thee hewed in pieces.
BOSOLA. Make not yourself such a promise of that life
   Which is not yours to dispose of.
CARDINAL. Who placed thee here?
BOSOLA. Her lust, as she intended.
CARDINAL. Very well:
   Now you know me for your fellow-murderer.
BOSOLA. And wherefore should you lay fair marble colors
   Upon your rotten purposes to me?
   Unless you imitate some that do plot great treasons,
   And when they have done, go hide themselves i' the graves
   Of those were actors in 't?
CARDINAL. No more; there is
   A fortune attends thee.
BOSOLA. Shall I go sue to Fortune any longer?
   'Tis the fool's pilgrimage.
CARDINAL. I have honors in store for thee.
BOSOLA. There are many ways that conduct to seeming honor,
   And some of them very dirty ones.
CARDINAL. Throw to the devil
   Thy melancholy. The fire burns well;
   What need we keep a stirring of 't, and make
   A greater smother? Thou wilt kill Antonio?
BOSOLA. Yes.

CARDINAL. Take up that body.

BOSOLA. I think I shall
Shortly grow the common bearer for churchyards.

CARDINAL. I will allow thee some dozen of attendants
To aid thee in the murder.

BOSOLA. O, by no means. Physicians that apply horse-leeches to any
rank swelling use to cut off their tails, that the blood may run
through them the faster: let me have no train when I go to shed
blood, lest it make me have a greater when I ride to the gallows.

CARDINAL. Come to me after midnight, to help to remove
That body to her own lodging: I'll give out
She died o' the plague; 'twill breed the less inquiry
After her death.

BOSOLA. Where's Castruccio, her husband?

CARDINAL. He's rode to Naples, to take possession
Of Antonio's citadel.

BOSOLA. Believe me, you have done a very happy turn.

CARDINAL. Fail not to come: there is the master-key
Of our lodgings; and by that you may conceive
What trust I plant in you.

BOSOLA. You shall find me ready.

Exit CARDINAL.

O poor Antonio, though nothing be so needful
To thy estate as pity, yet I find
Nothing so dangerous; I must look to my footing:
In such slippery ice-pavements men had need
To be frost-nailed well, they may break their necks.
The precedent's here afore me. How this man
Bears up in blood! seems fearless! Why, 'tis well: else;
Security some men call the suburbs of hell,
Only a dead wall between. Well, good Antonio,
I'll seek thee out; and all my care shall be
To put thee into safety from the reach
Of these most cruel biters that have got
Some of thy blood already. It may be,
I'll join with thee in a most just revenge:
The weakest arm is strong enough that strikes
With the sword of justice. Still methinks the duchess
Haunts me: there, there! — 'Tis nothing but my melancholy.
O Penitence, let me truly taste thy cup,
That throws men down only to raise them up!   [*Exit*

Scene III

A fortification at Milan.

    Enter ANTONIO *and* DELIO.

DELIO. Yond's the cardinal's window. This fortification
    Grew from the ruins of an ancient abbey;
    And to yond side o' the river lies a wall,
    Piece of a cloister, which in my opinion
    Gives the best echo that you ever heard,
    So hollow and so dismal, and withal
    So plain in the distinction of our words,
    That many have supposed it is a spirit
    That answers.
ANTONIO. I do love these ancient ruins.
    We never tread upon them but we set
    Our foot upon some reverend history:
    And, questionless, here in this open court,
    Which now lies naked to the injuries
    Of stormy weather, some men lie interred
    Loved the church so well, and gave so largely to 't,
    They thought it should have canopied their bones
    Till doomsday; but all things have their end:
    Churches and cities, which have diseases like to men,
    Must have like death that we have.
ECHO. "Like death that we have."
DELIO. Now the echo hath caught you.
ANTONIO. It groaned, methought, and gave
    A very deadly accent.
ECHO. "Deadly accent."
DELIO. I told you 'twas a pretty one: you may make it
    A huntsman, or a falconer, a musician,
    Or a thing of sorrow.
ECHO. "A thing of sorrow."
ANTONIO. Ay, sure, that suits it best.
ECHO. "That suits it best."
ANTONIO. 'Tis very like my wife's voice.
ECHO. "Ay, wife's voice."
DELIO. Come, let us walk further from 't.
    I would not have you go to the cardinal's to-night:
    Do not.
ECHO. "Do not."

DELIO. Wisdom doth not more moderate wasting sorrow
  Than time: take time for 't; be mindful of thy safety.
ECHO. "Be mindful of thy safety."
ANTONIO. Necessity compels me:
  Make scrutiny throughout the passages
  Of your own life, you'll find it impossible
  To fly your fate.
ECHO. "O, fly your fate."
DELIO. Hark! the dead stones seem to have pity on you,
  And give you good counsel.
ANTONIO. Echo, I will not talk with thee,
  For thou art a dead thing.
ECHO. "Thou art a dead thing."
ANTONIO. My duchess is asleep now,
  And her little ones, I hope sweetly: O Heaven,
  Shall I never see her more?
ECHO. "Never see her more."
ANTONIO. I marked not one repetition of the echo
  But that; and on the sudden a clear light
  Presented me a face folded in sorrow.
DELIO. Your fancy merely.
ANTONIO. Come, I'll be out of this ague,
  For to live thus is not indeed to live;
  It is a mockery and abuse of life:
  I will not henceforth save myself by halves;
  Lose all, or nothing.
DELIO. Your own virtues save you!
  I'll fetch your eldest son, and second you:
  It may be that the sight of his own blood
  Spread in so sweet a figure may beget
  The more compassion. However, fare you well.
  Though in our miseries Fortune have a part,
  Yet in our noble sufferings she hath none:
  Contempt of pain, that we may call our own.   [*Exeunt*

Scene IV

An apartment in the CARDINAL'S *palace.*

Enter CARDINAL, PESCARA, MALATESTI, RODERIGO, *and* GRISOLAN.

CARDINAL. You shall not watch to-night by the sick prince;
  His grace is very well recovered.

MALATESTI. Good my lord, suffer us.

CARDINAL. O, by no means;
  The noise, and change of object in his eye,
  Doth more distract him: I pray, all to bed;
  And though you hear him in his violent fit,
  Do not rise, I entreat you.

PESCARA. So, sir; we shall not.

CARDINAL. Nay, I must have you promise
  Upon your honors, for I was enjoined to 't
  By himself; and he seemed to urge it sensibly.

PESCARA. Let our honors bind this trifle.

CARDINAL. Nor any of your followers.

MALATESTI. Neither.

CARDINAL. It may be, to make trial of your promise,
  When he's asleep, myself will rise and feign
  Some of his mad tricks, and cry out for help,
  And feign myself in danger.

MALATESTI. If your throat were cutting,
  I'd not come at you, now I have protested against it.

CARDINAL. Why, I thank you.

GRISOLAN. 'Twas a foul storm to-night.

RODERIGO. The Lord Ferdinand's chamber shook like an osier.[57]

MALATESTI. 'Twas nothing but pure kindness in the devil,
  To rock his own child.

Exeunt all except CARDINAL.

CARDINAL. The reason why I would not suffer these
  About my brother, is, because at midnight
  I may with better privacy convey
  Julia's body to her own lodging. O, my conscience!
  I would pray now; but the devil takes away my heart
  For having any confidence in prayer.
  About this hour I appointed Bosola
  To fetch the body: when he hath served my turn,
  He dies.   [*Exit*

Enter BOSOLA.

BOSOLA. Ha! 'twas the cardinal's voice; I heard him name
  Bosola and my death. Listen; I hear one's footing.

Enter FERDINAND.

---

[57]A willow.

FERDINAND. Strangling is a very quiet death.

BOSOLA. [*Aside*] Nay, then, I see I must stand upon my guard.

FERDINAND. What say you to that? whisper softly; do you agree to 't? So; it must be done i' the dark: the cardinal would not for a thousand pounds the doctor should see it. [*Exit*

BOSOLA. My death is plotted; here's the consequence of murder.
We value not desert nor Christian breath,
When we know black deeds must be cured with death.

Enter ANTONIO *and* SERVANT.

SERVANT. Here stay, sir, and be confident, I pray:
I'll fetch you a dark lantern. [*Exit*

ANTONIO. Could I take him at his prayers,
There were hope of pardon.

BOSOLA. Fall right, my sword!— [*Stabs him*
I'll not give thee so much leisure as to pray

ANTONIO. O, I am gone! Thou hast ended a long suit
In a minute.

BOSOLA. What art thou?

ANTONIO. A most wretched thing,
That only have thy benefit in death,
To appear myself.

Re-enter SERVANT, *with a lantern.*

SERVANT. Where are you, sir?

ANTONIO. Very near my home.—Bosola!

SERVANT. O, misfortune!

BOSOLA. Smother thy pity, thou art dead else.—Antonio!
The man I would have saved 'bove mine own life!
We are merely the stars' tennis-balls, struck and bandied
Which way please them.—O good Antonio,
I'll whisper one thing in thy dying ear
Shall make thy heart break quickly! thy fair duchess and two sweet
children—

ANTONIO. Their very names
Kindle a little life in me.

BOSOLA. Are murdered.

ANTONIO. Some men have wished to die
At the hearing of sad things; I am glad
That I shall do 't in sadness:[58] I would not now
Wish my wounds balmed nor healed, for I have no use

---

[58]In earnest.

To put my life to. In all our quest of greatness,
Like wanton boys, whose pastime is their care,
We follow after bubbles blown in the air.
Pleasure of life, what is 't? only the good hours
Of an ague; merely a preparative to rest,
To endure vexation. I do not ask
The process of my death; only commend me
To Delio.
BOSOLA. Break, heart!
ANTONIO. And let my son fly the courts of princes.   [*Dies*
BOSOLA. Thou seem'st to have loved Antonio?
SERVANT. I brought him hither,
To have reconciled him to the cardinal.
BOSOLA. I do not ask thee that.
Take him up, if thou tender thine own life,
And bear him where the lady Julia
Was wont to lodge.—O, my fate moves swift;
I have this cardinal in the forge already;
Now I'll bring him to the hammer. O direful misprision![59]
I will not imitate things glorious,
No more than base; I'll be mine own example.—
On, on, and look thou represent, for silence,
The thing thou bear'st.   ·   [*Exeunt*

Scene V

Another apartment in the palace.

Enter CARDINAL, *with a book.*

CARDINAL. I am puzzled in a question about hell:
He says, in hell there's one material fire,
And yet it shall not burn all men alike.
Lay him by. How tedious is a guilty conscience!
When I look into the fish-ponds in my garden,
Methinks I see a thing armed with a rake,
That seems to strike at me.

Enter BOSOLA, *and* SERVANT *bearing* ANTONIO's *body.*

Now, art thou come?
Thou look'st ghastly:

---

[59]Mistake.

There sits in thy face some great determination
Mixed with some fear.
BOSOLA. Thus it lightens into action:
I am come to kill thee.
CARDINAL. Ha!—Help! our guard!
BOSOLA. Thou art deceived;
They are out of thy howling.
CARDINAL. Hold; and I will faithfully divide
Revenues with thee.
BOSOLA. Thy prayers and proffers
Are both unseasonable.
CARDINAL. Raise the watch! we are betrayed!
BOSOLA. I have confined your flight:
I'll suffer your retreat to Julia's chamber,
But no further.
CARDINAL. Help! we are betrayed!

Enter, above, PESCARA, MALATESTI, RODERIGO, *and* GRISOLAN.

MALATESTI. Listen.
CARDINAL. My dukedom for rescue!
RODERIGO. Fie upon his counterfeiting!
MALATESTI. Why, 'tis not the cardinal.
RODERIGO. Yes, yes, 'tis he:
But I'll see him hanged ere I'll go down to him.
CARDINAL. Here's a plot upon me; I am assaulted! I am lost,
Unless some rescue.
GRISOLAN. He doth this pretty well;
But it will not serve to laugh me out of mine honor.
CARDINAL. The sword's at my throat!
RODERIGO. You would not bawl so loud then.
MALATESTI. Come, come, let's go
To bed: he told us thus much aforehand.
PESCARA. He wished you should not come at him; but, believe 't,
The accent of the voice sounds not in jest:
I'll down to him, howsoever, and with engines
Force ope the doors.   [*Exit above*
RODERIGO. Let's follow him aloof,
And note how the cardinal will laugh at him.

Exeunt, above, MALATESTI, RODERIGO, *and* GRISOLAN.

BOSOLA. There's for you first,
'Cause you shall not unbarricade the door
To let in rescue.   [*Kills the* SERVANT

CARDINAL. What cause hast thou to pursue my life?
BOSOLA. Look there.
CARDINAL. Antonio!
BOSOLA. Slain by my hand unwittingly.
  Pray, and be sudden: when thou killed'st thy sister,
  Thou took'st from Justice her most equal balance,
  And left her naught but her sword.
CARDINAL. O, mercy!
BOSOLA. Now it seems thy greatness was only outward;
  For thou fall'st faster of thyself than calamity
  Can drive thee. I'll not waste longer time; there!   [*Stabs him*
CARDINAL. Thou hast hurt me.
BOSOLA. Again!   [*Stabs him again*
CARDINAL. Shall I die like a leveret,[60]
  Without any resistance?—Help, help, help!
  I am slain!

  Enter FERDINAND.

FERDINAND. The alarum! give me a fresh horse;
  Rally the vaunt-guard, or the day is lost.
  Yield, yield! I give you the honor of arms,
  Shake my sword over you; will you yield?
CARDINAL. Help me; I am your brother!
FERDINAND. The devil!
  My brother fight upon the adverse party!

  He wounds the CARDINAL, *and, in the scuffle, gives* BOSOLA *his death-wound.*

  There flies your ransom.
CARDINAL. O justice!
  I suffer now for what hath former bin:
  Sorrow is held the eldest child of sin.
FERDINAND. Now you're brave fellows. Caesar's fortune was harder
  than Pompey's; Caesar died in the arms of prosperity, Pompey at the
  feet of disgrace. You both died in the field. The pain's nothing: pain
  many times is taken away with the apprehension of greater, as the
  toothache with the sight of the barber that comes to pull it out:
  there's philosophy for you.
BOSOLA. Now my revenge is perfect.—Sink thou main cause
                                                           [*Kills* FERDINAND
  Of my undoing!—The last part of my life

---

[60]A hare in its first year.

Hath done me best service.

FERDINAND. Give me some wet hay; I am broken-winded.
I do account this world but a dog kennel:
I will vault credit and affect high pleasures
Beyond death.

BOSOLA. He seems to come to himself,
Now he's so near the bottom.

FERDINAND. My sister, O my sister! there's the cause on 't.
Whether we fall by ambition, blood, or lust,
Like diamonds we are cut with our own dust.   [Dies

CARDINAL. Thou hast thy payment too.

BOSOLA. Yes, I hold my weary soul in my teeth;
'Tis ready to part from me. I do glory
That thou, which stood'st like a huge pyramid
Begun upon a large and ample base,
Shalt end in a little point, a kind of nothing.

Enter below, PESCARA, MALATESTI, RODERIGO, *and* GRISOLAN.

PESCARA. How now, my lord!

MALATESTI. O sad disaster!

RODERIGO. How comes this?

BOSOLA. Revenge for the Duchess of Malfi murdered
By the Aragonian brethren; for Antonio
Slain by this hand; for lustful Julia
Poisoned by this man; and lastly for myself,
That was an actor in the main of all
Much 'gainst mine own good nature, yet i' the end
Neglected.

PESCARA. How now, my lord!

CARDINAL. Look to my brother:
He gave us these large wounds, as we were struggling
Here i' the rushes. And now, I pray, let me
Be laid by and never thought of.   [Dies

PESCARA. How fatally, it seems, he did withstand
His own rescue!

MALATESTI. Thou wretched thing of blood,
How came Antonio by his death?

BOSOLA. In a mist; I know not how;
Such a mistake as I have often seen
In a play. O, I am gone!
We are only like dead walls or vaulted graves,
That, ruined, yield no echo. Fare you well.
It may be pain, but no harm, to me to die

In so good a quarrel. O, this gloomy world!
In what a shadow, or deep pit of darkness,
Doth womanish and fearful mankind live!
Let worthy minds ne'er stagger in distrust *couplet*
To suffer death or shame for what is just:
Mine is another voyage.   [*Dies*
PESCARA. The noble Delio, as I came to the palace,
    Told me of Antonio's being here, and showed me
    A pretty gentleman, his son and heir.

Enter DELIO *and* ANTONIO'S SON.

MALATESTI. O sir, you come too late!
DELIO. I heard so, and
    Was armed for 't, ere I came. Let us make noble use
    Of this great ruin; and join all our force
    To establish this young hopeful gentleman
    In 's mother's right. These wretched eminent things
    Leave no more fame behind 'em, than should one
    Fall in a frost, and leave his print in snow;
    As soon as the sun shines, it ever melts,
    Both form and matter. I have ever thought
    Nature doth nothing so great for great men
    As when she's pleased to make them lords of truth:
    Integrity of life is fame's best friend,
    Which nobly, beyond death, shall crown the end.   [*Exeunt*

— the nobility of the Duchess shall live on